LARRY FRANCIS

LIVERS

Time & Place Prize Publishing
Chicago

Copyright © 2016 by Larry Francis

Author photo Copyright © 2015 by E.E.C.

Text set in Garamond

A Time & Place Prize Publication
Chicago

ISBN — 13: 978-0-69-263349-6

For my children,
Jacob, Ethan, and Arianna

LIVERS

For the king of Babylon stands at the parting of the way, at the head of the two ways, to use divination . . . he looks at the liver.
Ezekiel 21:21

1984
RIGHT LOBE
THE TORTOISE

I AM A MONSTER. And this is the story of my creation.

The story is a fragmented drama, its source material biased disparate annals. It is a collage, an uneven assemblage of accumulated interviews and notes, articles and manuscripts, photographs and recordings, memories and imagination. Picture a one-sided quilt, hand-stitched and irregular. It is an accursed tale of twisted personal prejudices and weathered partialities; it hangs on my bony shoulders like a homely, unwanted heirloom. The principal players in this singular prehistory—the quilt's patches—are two men and two women. They are—or were, at one time or another—related. More than kin, less than kind, as the saying goes. Call the rendering, then, four narratives, a quartered counterpane. Call it what you will. I won't object.

This unorthodox account of improbable origins is my

own. I am its sole chronicler and I alone—for fair or foul—bear ultimate responsibility. In the end, it is my story. I have done my best. And all a man—or a monster—can do is his best. I have sought the truth. And no history is bad so long as it is truthful.

Our curtain rises in the glare of a hospital: modern temple of record for white death and ruddy birth, callous incubator of hope and despair, past and future.

JOAN

"Poor, poor Walter," muttered Joan. "He never had a chance. Never saw it coming."

"Here, Mom, have some coffee. Two sugars. It'll help."

"Thank you. Have you heard from Philip?"

"He's on his way. Don't worry."

Joan sipped the weak warmth and worried. Somewhere in the belly of the building, in a room flooded with light and argot, a team of doctors and nurses and who-knows-who-else was doing their best to keep her husband alive.

"That stupid, stupid man," she said. Her thin frame trembled.

Seated next to her in the waiting room was her son, Mark. To her left sat Kate, Mark's girlfriend. No one else was waiting in the room. This made the space appear larger than it was. The walls were an ugly beige, the worn carpet an uglier blue. The avocado and orange Naugahyde chairs had angular, biting, wooden armrests. In a far corner a small television mounted to a fat black bracket broadcast MTV. The room smelled of hand sanitizer and fear.

Staring into the sepia at the bottom of her white plastic cup, Joan failed to see how this could be the end. Twenty-four years of marriage. He can't die, she told herself. Not now. The best is yet to come. That was the plan. That was *our* plan.

They'd met in college. She and Walter had shared notes and coffee and laughter, then ideas and kisses and dreams. The world was fresh and they fell in love. After graduation they married. Walter continued with his history studies: a master's at Northwestern and a doctorate at the University of Michigan. Joan kept house and got pregnant. The twins were born in Ann Arbor on a sunny spring day. Philip and Mark became her life.

Walter and Joan were giddy when Walter's dissertation on Babylonian hepatoscopy, *When We Looked to the Liver*, was published. His critical survey of ancient liver divination was never destined for the best-seller list; it was never going to make them famous or rich, but they had confidence the book would lead to a tenure track position at a good school. Joan believed they were on their way. She was young and figured she had everything she'd always wanted, everything she'd ever need.

Walter never got tenure. He declined the first few offers from second-tier schools while he waited for a perfect placement that never quite arrived. Walter, Joan, Philip and Mark—the Copelands—spent the next fifteen years tramping around the country, dependent on the short-term contracts of an aging adjunct history professor. Walter never authored another book. He put his energies into teaching and his family. Joan picked up clerical work where she could. They weren't wealthy but they were mostly happy. They managed. And then, one day, Walter was offered an associate professorship at Wallace College, a small liberal arts school in Delphi, Iowa, sometimes referred to as the Harvard of the Midwest, one of the hidden Ivies. A former Michigan classmate had become the history chair. They settled down. They bought a red and white two-story house. They acclimated to tractor traffic, endless farm fields and the smell of cow manure. Joan got a job in the admissions office. They lived. The twins grew into men. Philip received a mathematics scholarship to Caltech and Mark attended Wallace at a substantial discount because of his father the professor. They were on their way, again. The future swelled with promise. But now Walter lay dying.

"Mom, let me take that for you," said Mark reaching for her empty cup. Kate smiled. They make such a beautiful couple, thought Joan.

Philip thundered through the door. "What happened? Who's in charge here? Mother, are you okay? What have they done to Dad?"

"Oh, Philip, thank God you're here. Thank God you weren't in California. Thank God we're all together," cried Joan.

"Dad's in surgery," answered Mark. "We don't know anything yet."

Philip nodded. He saw the answer to his unasked question in his brother's eyes. He knew his

4

father was gone. He hugged his mother and nodded in Kate's direction.

"Mom, is there anything you need? Anything I can get for you?" he asked.

"No, I'm fine. Mark and Kate have been wonderful."

"Okay. I'm going to find out what's going on. Back in a minute."

Joan watched him march out the way he'd come. She turned and listened for the metallic rattle of the door. All morning she'd been adjusting to its grating sound, the distinctive racket of the latch bolt clack and lock, clack and lock, clack and lock. She knew that fate, sooner or later, would walk through that door and announce itself with a definitive, grave snap. Clack and lock. Yet there was no clack after Philip's departure. For an instant she thought the television might have muffled the door's noise. Or perhaps Philip had propped it open or had changed his mind about leaving. She turned to see what had prevented the sound. The door was open at an angle. A man in a brown delivery uniform, his chin to his chest, entered slowly.

Mark intercepted the man before he reached Joan. The two men exchanged hushed words. They turned toward the seated women.

"Mom, this is Marvin Plotkin. He'd like to talk to you, that is, if it's okay."

Joan saw the man had been crying. His hands shook. She assumed he was someone Walter had been kind to, someone he had helped. She welcomed hearing good things about her husband. She had no objections to sharing her pain.

"Ma'am, I am so terribly sorry," started Plotkin. "If there was any way to go back, any way to undo it I . . . I've gone over it a thousand times in my head and there was nothing I could've done . . . if only . . . I'm so, so, terribly sorry."

Joan was confused. Mark intervened.

"He's the truck driver."

The man again lowered his head. "If there was anything I could've done. If there's anything I *can* do for you or your family, I—"

Marvin was pleading. Joan wasn't listening. She eyed the logo on his shirt: a green cartoon turtle sprinting on two stout legs. She had seen it before. Where? Why was it so familiar? Yes, of course, the same logo was painted on the truck that had run over her husband. The red-hatted turtle was holding a package and smiling. What on odd logo for a delivery company, she thought, a fleet turtle, an oxymoron.

"I didn't see him. He came out of nowhere. I know there's nothing I can say to make it better. I just had to tell you how sorry I am. It's all I can think to do. I'm so sorry."

Mark and Kate held hands and their eyes filled with tears. Joan asked the man to sit down and thanked him.

"It wasn't your fault," she said. "My husband wasn't paying attention. He was so scatterbrained. He *is* so scatterbrained. He was warning me about a stupid crack in the sidewalk when he tripped into the street. 'Step on a crack.' He was making a joke. There was nothing you could've done. There was nothing anyone could've done. It was an accident."

As the driver spoke, begging for forgiveness, repeating how sorry he was, Joan returned to the untroubled turtle on his tight shirt. There was something intriguing and distracting about it. She was mesmerized. It means something, she thought.

Marvin stood to leave and took her hand. She thanked him again as he said they were all in his prayers and always would be. The door closed behind him. Clack and lock. Then, suddenly, she understood the allure of the turtle.

"What an unfortunate man," she mumbled. "There was nothing he could've done."

Remembering, Joan leaned back and squeezed her eyelids shut. Yes, that night in New Orleans. Nowhere else but New Orleans, she thought. From the outset she had found the city eerie, unsettling. But Walter had secured a two year contract at Tulane and back in those days that meant stability.

It was night, warm and windy. The history department had organized a kind of fund-raising fair. She hadn't wanted to go. Walter had had to beg her. He'd even arranged for a baby-sitter for the boys. It was rare for them to get out alone, together. The 'fair' was little more than a Lucky Dog cart, two beer tents—one serving beer, the other Hurricanes—and three historically themed sideshows hidden behind cheap black curtains. There was a Haitian voodoo booth, a mock guillotining, and Walter's contribution: an overdone Greek oracle attraction, where for three dollars you could enter and have the three masked Fates issue three personal prophecies. 'A dollar a peek for your future.' Walter was enjoying himself and halfway through her second Hurricane so was Joan. Walter wanted to visit all the diversions but Joan deemed them morbid. He implored her to at least see his. "It's for a good cause," he said.

Behind the black drapes three hooded figures huddled behind large fake rocks. An amplified voice echoed from the makeshift grotto.

"You dare to learn your fate from the three daughters of Nyx?"

Walter answered, "We do."

"Oh, no! *We* most certainly do not. Not me. Just him." said Joan.

"Fine, just me," said Walter. "We only paid three dollars anyway."

"Silence!"

Joan was spooked by the voice's tone.

The first cloaked figure stood and spoke:

"A rapid tortoise to the skull shall mean your demise."

"Did you say a *rabid* tortoise?" teased Walter.

"Rapid. Fast. A fast tortoise," clarified the Fate, stuttering with anger.

"Oh, okay. Rapid."

"Silence!"

After a pause, the second specter rose:

"One son will be the death of the other."

At the oblique mention of her children, Joan dropped Walter's arm and ran from the booth. Outside, in the laughter and the lights, she waited.

"Why'd you leave?" Walter asked. "Too hokey? Sorry. Not very realistic, was it?"

"I fail to see the pleasure in pronouncements of death and misery," she said.

Walter laughed. "Joan, it's a show. They're graduate students. Listen, if they could really see the future they'd be doing better in my class. And that turtle to the head bit? It's the infamous Aeschylus legend. Author of the *Oresteia*? I'm sure it's familiar. No? Well, here it is. As a disclaimer, keep in mind there are no reliable sources for the life or death of Aeschylus. This is all legend. Nevertheless, it is said that the famous playwright was killed by a tortoise dropped by an eagle which mistook his bald head for a rock suitable for shattering the shell of the reptile. Allegedly he died on the spot. Out cold, forever. It's apocryphal. It's ridiculous. My favorite part of the story is the attribution of intent to the eagle. Priceless. It's a myth. Most likely, my students were referring to my expanding bald spot. It's actually moderately funny. Don't be upset. It's all in the name of charity, all in good fun."

"I don't find it charitable. Nor is it good or fun. I don't like to think about such things, Walter. You know that."

"Fine. Have another Hurricane or I'll tell you what the third prophecy was."

"Don't you dare!"

New Orleans vanished with a clack and lock.

"He's dead," said Philip.

"A tortoise to the skull," whispered Joan.

"Dad's dead," he repeated.

A flood of professionals in diverse uniforms entered behind Philip with a clack and lock, clack and lock, some wore scrubs, some wore white lab coats, some wore expensive suits. Deluged in condolences, whys and wherefores, the family was escorted into a second, much smaller, more comfortable room, where the chairs were made of real leather and the walls were painted robin's egg blue. A Bible, not a television, decorated the far corner. Ornate tissue dispensers were everywhere. After a few minutes the doctors and nurses left to fight other battles. Death never rests. The grief counselor and her silent assistant remained.

Joan sat composed. The shock of the accident, its surreal suddenness, had subsided, replaced by the immutable finality of death. She had witnessed the accident. She knew it was bad. And now there was nothing else she could do. The grief counselor, a tallish woman with enormous brown eyes, cautioned against suppressing her emotions. Joan felt she was being asked to perform. Philip became angry. Mark and Kate were both busy wiping away tears.

"Do you believe in fate?" Joan asked the grief counselor.

"I believe everything happens for a reason. But more often than not we can't see or don't know the reason."

"What's the value of an unknown reason?"

"I wish I had answers for you, Mrs. Copeland. Please understand that I am here for you, day or night, should you ever want to talk," said the grief counselor handing her a business card.

Philip snatched the card. "If we need you, we'll call. Thank you."

"Mom, it couldn't hurt to talk to somebody," said Mark.

"I remember when my mother died," said Kate, "I didn't cry for three days. Then I cried for a whole two weeks. Once it started it wouldn't stop. I was a basket case. But we're all different."

"She has us," declared Philip. "She doesn't need to talk to someone who never knew him. She has us. She has everything she needs."

"Certainly, and it's only in the event you wish to . . . it isn't compulsory, after all. It's just that we have experience in this unfortunate and inevitable life event. And sharing, talking, with a third party, often assists in the grieving process."

"We have your card," said Philip.

"Yes, you do," said the grief counselor. She paused and cleared her throat. "There are also the practical matters to consider."

"Like?" asked Mark.

"First, do you wish to view the deceased, have a few private moments, say farewell?"

Kate winced. Philip spoke.

"As I understand it, the accident and your hospital's brutally unsuccessful attempts to save his life have left my father in a less than photogenic condition. I think it would be better to remember him as he was."

"Philip is right," said Joan. "Mark, if you want to go."

"No, I'll stay here with you."

"If that is your wish," said the tall woman. She signaled to her assistant who excused himself and left.

"And there are other arrangements to be made," she started.

"I'll take care of that," said Philip. "My mother has been through enough today. She doesn't need to be tortured by your bureaucracy on top of everything else."

Mark kissed Kate and stood. He walked Philip to the far corner, a hand on his brother's shoulder.

Joan watched her sons bicker in whispers about the arrangements and her thoughts turned to the Fates' second prophecy. '*One son will be the death of the other.*' Walter is gone. All I have are my boys, my two boys. And one of them will be next. Unless I can prevent it, she thought. Kate moved next to her. Joan took her slender hand and looked again at her sons. Two decades and how alike they still looked, yet how different, identical but not.

"Mark, please let Philip handle all that. You come here by me and Kate. Maybe you could take us home. Philip, does that work for you?"

"Of course, Mom. It works. No problem at all. I'll see you at home, later."

PHILIP

Philip possessed a prosaic mind. In this he was unlike his abstract, liberal arts father. So it was unsurprising that of all his dad's ancient stories—a thousand bedtime tales of golden fleeces, great floods, wars and auguries, the melding of myth, legend, love and antiquity—Philip remembered but one pragmatic sentiment. It was a history lesson he would never forget. His father, closing a meaty, well-thumbed book, had said, "Boys, all history is selection. It is but one possible story among many. Every historian chooses his own history."

Philip chose his father's death as the beginning of his estrangement from Mark. That's when, he decided, his brother's resentment became overt. It's when the rivalry was made manifest.

In my collection of digital audio files there's an old MP3 confessing as much. It was recorded long before I was conceived. On it Philip declares, 'The twinship started with me. It was unequal from the beginning. And my brother could never forgive me for being the first one out. But, accepted or not, I am the elder. It is a fact he has always been bitter about. It became obvious when our father died.'

Philip took over. He assumed control. He was decisive. He made the unhappy arrangements, alone, with calculation and dispatch. His father's body was transferred and incinerated by the local funeral home. A squat brass urn with curved symmetrical handles was selected as repository for Walter's ashes. A small nondenominational service was organized and publicized. Philip managed policemen, college administrators and insurance agents. Joan thanked him for jobs well done. She called him her hero. Mark, sitting on the living room sofa, tucked between the women, his arm entwined with Kate's, thanked him too. "Don't know what we would've done without you, Philip." Kate smiled. She was very pretty. In some ways Mark was luckier than he deserved, thought Philip.

There wasn't much to be thankful for that bleak Thanksgiving of 1984. It was chilly and snowless, dun. Canadian winds whipped south without challenge. The dirt turned hard as stone. Philip hadn't been home in almost two years. California was far away and he was always too busy. Iowa had little hold on him. He had returned a different person, an adult, one greeted by his father's death. And he had been charged with picking up the pieces.

He'd only arrived the night before, too late for the family dinner. He'd barely spoken to his parents. They were in their pajamas when he got in. He pumped his father's hand twice and hugged his mother before they retired for the night. He and Mark stayed up late talking about their studies, their mutual friends and their lives, catching up. Philip talked mostly about programming, Mark mostly mooned over Kate.

He slept late. The others were gone when he awoke. After a quick shower he answered the ringing telephone and rushed to the hospital. His wet hair stiffened in the cold Iowa air.

The check on his mother was brief and he found the operating room where they were working on Walter Copeland just as the doctors were giving up. He reached the OR in time to watch them surrender and switch off the machines. A nurse stopped him from going any farther. "I'm sorry. We did our best," she said. A doctor came out, removed his blue cloth hat, darkened by perspiration, and told Philip, "The head trauma was too severe. I'm sorry." Philip was never quite able to remember whether or not he had thanked them, probably not. He ran back to the waiting room to be the first to tell his mother the bad news. The task was his. It was his duty.

Apart from the Pasadena warmth, Philip missed his California coursework. He missed his colleagues and his professors. He missed their optimistic visions for the future. They—he among them—were in the vanguard of science and technology. It was exciting. Fifteen hundred miles away, beyond the Rocky Mountains and the Great Divide, freshened by the salty Pacific Ocean, they discussed, worked and dreamed. Every slow, dull minute in Delphi reminded him that he was falling behind. There was no urgency in Iowa, no ambition, only relations, only the frozen past.

Walter's wishes, according to Joan, were that his ashes be scattered to the four winds. Philip lacked his late father's romanticism but respected the request. Mark suggested the bluffs overlooking Lake Red Rock. Philip set the date.

It was supposed to be just family, thought Philip, as Kate slipped in next to him in the sedan. Mark pushed her toward the middle, closer, and slammed the door. Joan waited in the driver's seat tapping the steering wheel.

"All set, Mom," said Mark, squeezing close to Kate. Joan checked her mirrors. The urn rested in the front passenger seat. Mark suggested securing it with the safety belt but was overruled when Philip deemed the suggestion ridiculous and redundant.

No one spoke during the brief drive to the lake.

Kate caught Joan's bloodshot eyes in the rearview mirror and smiled. Philip looked out the window without seeing. Mark caressed Kate's hand in his.

Atop the cliffs the arctic winds swirled. The lake was white with little waves. Philip hoped the scattering wouldn't take long. Mark proposed they each make a speech. Joan vetoed the idea saying Walter wouldn't have wanted them to freeze to death. She told the boys to each grab an urn handle and she would unfasten the top. They could then sow the ashes however they chose. Philip tried to calculate the direction of the wind but failed. It seemed to be coming from everywhere, all at once. Mark grabbed a brass handle and waited. Philip suggested they coordinate their movements. Mark laughed and said, "Just shake it, Philip." They nodded. Joan removed the lid. They inched closer to the bluff's edge and inverted the urn, emptying its contents. For a second or two, the ashes, shimmering high in the sunlight, rose and spread sideways, lifted by the wild wind, before a second, stronger gust hurled the remains back toward the twins. Kate gasped. Joan smiled. Mark laughed. Philip glowered. Like dogs, the boys tried to shake themselves clean. Paternal ash fell in clumps from Philip's head. Mark laughed a second time. No one spoke on the ride back. Kate rode in front. The urn went in the trunk.

The next morning Philip stood at the kitchen counter planning his exit strategy and listening to the coffee brew. A twinge of guilt made him consider the possibility that his mother still hadn't accepted the loss of her husband. He still hadn't seen her cry. What kind of person abandons his mother? he asked himself. Lost in youthful meditation on morality and mortality he stared out over the sink through the latticed window and watched the breeze shake loose the last of the autumn leaves. Freedom is a mirage, he concluded, responsibility a tether. A hand reached around his waist and found his crotch.

"What the—"

He seized the prowler's delicate wrist and spun around.

"Oh, Christ! Philip! It's you. I am so sorry. I thought you were Mark," Kate apologized. "You're wearing his sweatshirt and from the back you look—"

Philip released her hand. She froze. Her breath was warm and sweet, her perfume a blend of baby powder and candy; a few strands of her long blonde hair rested on his shoulder.

"I'm low on clothes. It was supposed to be a weekend visit. I hadn't expected such a long stay, not to mention being plastered in ashes. Mark's in the shower. I'm sure he'll be down in a minute. Coffee?"

"Uh, no. Thank you. I wouldn't have . . . but your mother told me Mark was in here. And, Christ, you two look so much alike. You should wear nametags or something."

"We may look alike, but I assure you we are very different."

"I believe you," she said.

"You should."

Neither moved. And, for several long seconds, neither spoke. Philip lost himself in her green eyes. She met his gaze and then looked down. Her eyebrows rose and she looked up.

"Listen, Mark doesn't need to know about this," she said. "It was just a silly misunderstanding and he's so sensitive and this is a difficult time and all. Well, you know."

"Yes, I know."

Joan exploded into the kitchen asking if the coffee was ready. Kate and Philip separated.

"Oh, Philip, it's you. I thought you were Mark."

Philip poured his mother coffee. She sat down and fanned away the rising steam.

"Kate, dear, I owe you an apology. I thought Philip was the one in the shower. I don't know how I could've made such a mistake. You'd think I'd know my own boys by now. Then again these have been trying days. They have taken their toll. And then the nights, the long, restless nights. I haven't slept very well, perhaps that's it. Thank goodness I've had Philip and Mark here. I can't imagine what shape I'd be in without them."

Later, the Copeland twins went to the movies for a matinee showing of *The Terminator*. There was nothing else to do on a lazy Tuesday afternoon in Delphi. Kate was supposed to join them but changed her mind.

"I don't think she would've liked it anyway," said Mark. "It was totally a guy movie."

"I'm a guy and I thought it sucked," said Philip.

Diagonally, they crossed the small town square. The sun was already low in the western sky creating a beard shadow on the bust of a founding father. On the far side of the square a young man in baggy, greasy overalls and a green mesh trucker's cap entered the townie bar. Country music, laughter and cigarette smoke escaped.

"It's apropos we're talking about masculinity because," said Mark, "it was one of the big themes of the movie. The film was essentially an argument that being a man requires more than having the body of a man. We are more than our flesh."

"I don't know what you're babbling about," said Philip. "The film was about one thing and one thing only: the danger of artificial intelligence. And, while I appreciate the nod to the coming age of thinking computers, I found it childishly unbelievable and uninteresting."

"Uninteresting? It was all action. It was one long chase scene."

"I mean uninteresting from a scientific perspective. We're never going to lose control of our technology. It simply cannot happen. It's not believable. Unless, I suppose, you know nothing about the subject, unless you're an idiot."

"I think the real reason you didn't like the movie is because you identified with the Terminator. You wanted him to win, didn't you? You expected him to win."

"Maybe," said Philip. "He was tenacious."

They turned off Main Street and stood opposite the Grill, the college bar. Mark suggested they go in for a pitcher.

"Come on, we can play pool. It'll be like old times."

Philip hadn't been inside the Grill in years.

Walter had introduced the boys to Earl, the owner and sole bartender, when they moved to Delphi. The brothers drank there before they were legal. Their dad used it as a second office. And because it was where Mark met Kate, the brothers had dubbed it the Girll. Philip was confident nothing inside had changed. He could picture it without effort: the two creeping ceiling fans; the scratched and smudged Old Style mirrors; the faded Budweiser lampshades; the missing segment of foot rail; the pool table, one leg raised by cardboard coasters, its thin felt burnt and torn; the same old dumpy jukebox with the same old overplayed songs; the wobbly, creaking barstools, their seats leaking dirty, yellow foam; the tall wooden booths vandalized into totems, the over-scrawled red brick wall. The Girll.

"No thanks. Not today," he answered.

The wind died. Mark claimed he could smell winter approaching.

"Let's go for a long walk, a really long walk," said Mark.

"Why?" asked Philip.

"Why? Because it's a beautiful afternoon, a beautiful day, a one of a kind day that when it's gone is gone forever. And it is ours to experience. Right now. We should revel in such a gift."

"You're nuts."

"It's a walk, Philip. It's just a walk."

"We don't walk in California," he replied. "We drive. I'm going home to check on Mom."

They parted in front of the Hardee's.

His mother was reading when Philip entered.

"Mark's out walking," he told her.

"Yes, he does that," said Joan.

Philip shook his head and sat down. He was about to tell his mother it was time he got back to California. She spoke first.

"Philip, I want to thank you for everything you've done. You've gone above and beyond. But I think it's time for you to get back to school. I'm sure you're very busy. And your graduation is in the spring. You've been inconvenienced enough."

"Are you sure?"

"I am positive. We will all miss you, of course, but we'll manage. Life goes on."

"I do have a lot to do. I'm behind schedule."

"Then it's settled. You will return to California as soon as possible. But before you go would you help me with one more thing."

Philip started packing and planning in his head. He'd already missed the day's flight to LA. Perhaps he could get a seat on tomorrow's. His mother continued.

"I was wondering if you would speak with Mark and ask him if he wouldn't mind moving back into the house with me, temporarily. I know he's nearby and with his friends. But, at least for a while, it would be nice not to be alone in this big house."

"Sure, Mom, I'll talk to him. He'll do it. He'll move back."

That night, after their mother had gone to bed, the twins talked. Philip told Mark he was leaving in the morning.

"It's time," he said. "I've stayed long enough.

21

There's nothing left for me to do here."

Mark agreed, thanked him for everything and wished him well.

"Mark," began Philip, "Mom wants you to move back in."

"I'm twenty-one years old," said Mark. "And I'm just around the corner. I'll visit her every day. I promise."

"It'll only be for a while, just until she processes what happened, until she gets used to being by herself."

"She'll never get used to being by herself if I'm here."

"It's Mom. And it's not like you've got anything better to do. It's not like you've got plans."

"Oh, I get it. I understand. Because you're out to save or destroy the world with your computers or whatever, it's my job to stay at home with the women."

"You said it, not me."

"A man is defined by his character not by what he does."

"Remind me again, for the record, what do you do anyway? What's your major?" asked Philip.

"General studies."

"Perfect, you can study things generally from Mom's house. And your flawless character will remain intact."

The next morning Mark offered to drive him to the airport, but Philip, sensing an insincere gesture and not wanting his mother left alone, insisted on taking the bus to Des Moines. The four of them gathered in Delphi's tiny white waiting room watching for the coach. There were only two folding chairs. The boys stood. The concrete floor was sticky and gray. Joan was relaxed. Mark looks upset, thought Philip. When the bus rounded the corner he stood and shook his brother's limp hand. He hugged Kate. He kissed his mother on both cheeks. Philip boarded the bus and waved to them from a scratched window. He was glad to be leaving Iowa. He wouldn't miss much.

MARK

Mark took his father's death hard, harder than anyone else. He was, after all, the youngest. And there was no doubt that he possessed a sensitive soul. He had always been more spiritual, more metaphysical, than his brother. But the real reason Walter's death caused him so much pain was what had happened the evening before, the way father and son had left things.

At their last supper, a few hours before Philip's arrival, over dry roasted chicken, mashed potatoes, boiled green beans and anticipation, an innocent question led to a final argument.

"Has Philip said what he's going to do after graduation?" asked Joan.

"He says he plans to leave Southern California with a couple of his classmates and head up north," answered Walter, "south of San Francisco, I think, the Santa Clara valley. That's the hub for all this computing business. They're going to start up their own company, something to do with computer protection and security. I'm sure he'll tell us all about it when he gets here."

If there was one thing Mark was certain of it was that Philip had a meticulously detailed plan for his future. And he was also fairly certain, sooner or later, they'd hear about it. He asked his mother for more green beans.

"What about you?" asked Walter. "What does life have in store for you come June?"

"If I knew that, Dad, I'd be a rich man," Mark joked.

"Seriously."

"I'm not sure. I'm thinking about grad school but it's a huge commitment and I don't know what I'd study. I don't think I'm there yet."

"No, I don't believe you are," said his father.

"I guess I'll look for a job, though the market isn't great. Oh, Mr. Purcell said I could stay on at the student union. So, at least in the short term, there's no real pressure. I'm happy here."

"A job is one thing, Mark. A career is quite another. You didn't go to college to work in a student union for the rest of your life."

"No, I didn't. I went there to learn. And I've learned a lot."

"Most students learn what they want to do with their lives."

Mark was glib. "I am not most students."

"Clearly."

Joan tried to change the subject by offering

more chicken. Neither man took the bait.

"Dad, let me ask you then, what should I do if I'm not passionate about one single thing? Is it my fault I don't love history like you or programming like Philip?"

"Do something," answered his father. "Make a plan at least, even if it turns out to be a pipe-dream. Plans can change, you know. It's allowed. But make a start."

"Planning requires choosing and any choice made now would be false and dishonest. It would be artifice. It would be for show, for other people. It would not be for me. It would not be living. And I want to live."

"We all want to live, Mark. Don't think you're different from the rest of us."

"More potatoes?" asked Joan.

"I'm not saying I'm special," replied Mark, "just sincere." Then he decided on another tack. "Take music, for example. Have you ever listened to a song and felt moved to the point the hairs on your body stand like wire and your entire existence fills the present so thoroughly that nothing else seems to matter?"

"Of course I have, that's the power of art."

"There's a song out now, 'Pink Houses.' And it gets me every time. It puts me in that numinous 'now.' I admit I don't know enough about music to say whether I'm responding to a chord progression, a catchy melody, the lyrics, the singer's enthusiasm or a combination. I only know that I feel alive, really alive, at certain moments during that song. And it isn't just

25

contemporary music. I react the same way to some of Chopin's works. And to Beethoven's. In fact it isn't only music. It's everything. It's in a child's laugh. It's in the breath of the breeze in my face. It's in the fragrance of a flower. It's in Kate's touch. It's in the taste and texture of my favorite foods. It's in an act of kindness. It can be in almost anything. You know, this probably sounds strange, but sometimes I feel the urge to lick the surface of a wall just to feel the sensation on my tongue. I want to experience it all. I am happy, content, living. It doesn't matter what I do as long as I feel alive. I want to live in the present, always. I want it all, every single second of it. I want to experience everything, moment after beautiful moment. That's what I'm passionate about."

"Mark, that's hedonism. You're an epicurean."

"No, hedonism and epicureanism are about pleasure. This is not about pleasure, though I'd cop to a charge of solipsism. This is about something else. It's about feeling and filling existence, the good and the bad, the pleasure and the pain. It's about living. I want to live."

"Good luck with that. No one's going to pay you to sit around and live."

"I don't need much. I have life. I will live."

"Don't be an idiot," said Walter. "Life is cruel to idiots. Joan, I've lost my appetite. I'll see you upstairs. Mark, we'll discuss this another time."

But there was no other time. Mark never spoke to his father again. Early the next morning he left for a walk and to see Kate. He was naked and breathless when his mother, crying, called from the hospital.

They rushed to her side. His mother was a mess. She was shaking. She was incoherent. "No one's answering the telephone at home," she cried. "No one's there." She was afraid. He understood there had been some kind of accident. He didn't dare leave to find out from the doctors how bad things were. He expected the worst. He asked Kate to call Philip. He served coffee. He turned on the television. As a distraction he criticized the room's décor. He exchanged long, sympathetic, confused glances with Kate. He held his mother's hand and repeated over and over that everything would be all right even though he didn't believe it himself. "The worst is over. He's in good hands." He calmed her down. Her tears dried. Then she spoke about the accident. She told them about the terrible crunch of the collision. She admitted survival was impossible. She insisted her husband was dead. Mark kept her calm. She became stoic. She whispered a passive good-bye. "Poor, poor Walter." She asked again for Philip. "He's on his way. Don't worry." Mark told her to wait for the doctors. They were sure to have some news soon. He spoke to the man who struck his father. He listened to him—that sorry Plotkin—beg for forgiveness. Mark held her hand. He was there for his mother. He comforted her. He brought her back. But it was Philip who announced Walter was dead.

Mark broke down in the upstairs bathroom, his emotional strength exhausted. He could no longer keep his heartache in check. Downstairs, Kate and Joan drank tea and remembered Walter. Mark could almost make out their mumbled words amid his sobs. Over and over he replayed the argument. He had not been nice. He regretted not the stance but the tone. He had been disrespectful and flip. It was not how he had vowed to live. He had caused bad blood when it wasn't necessary and now there was nothing he could do to fix it. He could not make it right. It was a bitter lesson. He looked in the lighted mirror and wiped his eyes. He combed his hair with his fingers and said "I'm sorry" out loud. Then he rejoined the women and pretended he was fine. He was sitting between them on the sofa laughing when Philip returned and told them everything had been taken care of. They all gave Philip his due praise.

Mark had always suspected that Philip thought he was the better brother. Their dad's death merely confirmed the notion. Philip's elevation was almost a rite of succession, a unilateral validation of something that until then had merely been implied. He was now the presumed head of the Copeland clan, no need for discussion, there was never any question. It was his birthright.

There's an entertaining passage in Mark's papers about this presumed superiority and its inevitability. The excerpt is revealing on many levels. In typically protracted fashion he writes, 'Often conflating or confusing serendipity and achievement, like a superstitious athlete, my big brother firmly believes, to this very day, that he somehow willed himself firstborn, that owing to a felicitous fusion of unparalleled newborn strength, an innate sense of direction and a freakish determination—in addition to what I humorously term a premature thirst for adventure—he purposefully burst forth first, headlong, into life's blinding glare. He would rush to add, modestly, I am certain, that he did this, in part, to protect me, the younger, the weaker, the second *son. My brother gulped his first breath of air two hundred seconds before me and because of this, he believes, I must forever swim in his afterbirth.'*

Sometimes the 'little' brother bested the 'big' brother. The night they first met Kate—the night the Grill became the Girll—was one such time.

It was freshman year, 1981, and Philip was home for Christmas break. A thick layer of new snow muffled the streets of Delphi. Most Wallace students had left for the holidays and the Grill was quiet. Inside and toasty, Mark and Philip shared a pitcher of beer and shot pool. They split four games. Mark had accidentally potted the eight ball to lose the last. Philip raved about California. Mark, without envy, was happy for him. They debated having another pitcher when Kate and her friend, Meg, walked into the bar

It is less awkward if I let Mark describe the event. This is again from his notes. He writes, 'Kate was easily the most devastatingly beautiful girl I had ever seen and her beauty—her ethereal, graceful, insouciant, indescribable beauty—filled me, surprisingly, with a profound, poignant, existential sadness. From across the room, without so much as a glance in my direction, she broke my heart. And I was plunged into sadness. I was sad for a beauty that would inevitably be disfigured by unyielding time. I was sad for all the delusive men who would seek to possess her. I was sad for average Meg. (For who would ever notice her hidden in Kate's corona?) I was also sad for Kate herself because there would come a day, one tragic day, when she would realize her beauty was a curse. But, ultimately, selfishly, I was sad for myself because there, standing before me, was everything I had ever wanted. And I was powerless. I felt possessed. I knew I was in love, forever. I figured we all were: me, Philip, Meg, even Earl, timeless, behind the bar. We all loved her. Everyone loved her. I never for one instant dreamed she would love me back.'

With the confidence of a conquistador, Philip invited Venus and her friend to join the mortal Copeland brothers. He ordered drinks and directed the conversation. He proclaimed California was the Promised Land and computers would change the world. Mark was quiet. He listened. He heard Kate was also a freshman at Wallace and her dad was the manager at the student union. He heard Meg was studying art history. Kate was going to be an actress. The two girls were dorm mates. Philip boasted that their dad was a professor. Kate whispered to Meg and they both giggled. For some reason Mark giggled too. Philip bought more drinks. Two upperclassmen, smoking cigarettes and shaking off snow, came in and sat at the bar. Mark asked the girls if they'd like to hear some music.

"I'll go with you," said Kate.

"Do you like REO?" asked Mark.

"Love 'em."

"Me too."

"You and your brother look so much alike. It's uncanny."

"Yeah, I know. We're not the same though."

"I can tell."

After the girls left Philip began damage control.

"The only reason you got her number is you two go to the same school. She figured I wouldn't be around."

"Probably," said Mark. But somehow he knew Kate was to be his forever.

Philip moped through the New Year. He didn't like to lose and he couldn't wait to get back to California. The morning of his departure he practically sprinted out of the house to catch his bus.

The ash reaction was another time the younger twin prevailed. Obscured by their father's charcoal cloud, the identical-looking brothers responded as if they were different species. The better brother, thought Mark, laughing. "Philip, at least tell me you had your mouth closed," he said flicking off ash, watching his brother fume. Mark wasn't irritated. He was grateful. He didn't believe in the supernatural—his philosophy was telluric, tangible—yet, when his dad's dust suddenly, in midair, reversed course and enveloped them, he couldn't help but take it as a sign. He couldn't help but laugh. It was a reminder not to dwell in the past. It was as if Walter, with one final gesture, had said, 'Here I am boys, your one and only father. I'll always be a part of you. I'll always be with you.' How could you not laugh? thought Mark. So he let that last argument go. He believed he had been released. Philip, on the other hand, was merely dirty.

The night before he flew to California Philip ordered Mark to move back in with Joan. Mark would have done anything for his mother, all she had to do was

31

ask. If she needed him, he would be there. No one had to tell him what to do, all they had to do was ask politely. Philip's attitude was unnecessary; his involvement was unnecessary. He was leaving. He had no say in the matter. Philip seemed to enjoy belittling Mark. He was mean. Mark fought back. Any remaining cords of childhood closeness were severed that night.

Mark needed Kate after Philip left. And she was there for him. They went straight from the bus station to his apartment to pack up his things. Kate was a great organizer. She knew what to pack and what to leave behind. "After all," she said, "you don't know how long you'll be there. It might just be a day or two, maybe a week. And you can always come back for more." As a few fat flakes of snow fell they carried the two neatly packed bags three blocks to Joan's. Kate stayed with Mark the rest of the day and into the evening.

After Joan had gone up to bed they turned on the television and canoodled on the couch. They sought solace in intimacy. Too much was raw. Kate stopped mid-kiss, reached into her back pocket and withdrew a crinkled beer bottle label. She handed it to Mark and began unbuttoning his shirt.

"This entitles me to anything, you know."

"But my mom is upstairs."

"I know. Don't think about her. Think about me."

"Okay. Okay. Wait. Wait. One second."

Mark turned up the volume on the television and helped Kate out of her jeans.

KATE

Kate and Mark had been dating for three years when Walter died. She knew Mark's parents well. She liked them. In fact she spent more time at their house than she did her dorm. She liked it there. She enjoyed the idea of being in a professor's home. It was like playing a part in a movie. She called Mark's parents—at their insistence—by their first names. She helped Joan with the dishes. She laughed at Walter's peculiar, unfunny historical jokes. They ate suppers together. They confided in her. And in return she kept Mark happy. She was a good girlfriend, a damn good girlfriend. And a good girlfriend goes to the hospital when her boyfriend's dad is dying. It's what good girlfriends do.

Mark was an absolute wreck but he was trying, for Joan's sake, to hide his feelings. Joan was in bad shape too, at least when they first arrived at the hospital. Kate thought it was all very normal behavior for a catastrophe. But after the truck driver left, the room changed. Joan changed. She became calm. It was like it was all suddenly okay, like it made sense that her husband had been hit by a truck. It was as if Joan had flipped a before-and-after switch. And the after setting didn't include her husband. The change was too dramatic. It was too sudden. It was frightening. It was the first time Kate had ever been afraid of anyone. And she couldn't—she would never—share such thoughts with Mark. It wouldn't be fair. Neither would it make any difference. When Philip charged through the waiting room door with

33

news of Walter's death the announcement was almost anticlimactic.

From a theatrical standpoint Kate appreciated Philip's flair for the dramatic. As an actress it was something she knew about firsthand. It was showmanship, though in Philip's case it wasn't an act. For him it was his way of being, as natural as his tallness. Philip was dramatic and confident because he believed himself important and definitive. He was the epitome of method. His bravado was a symptom. It took her years to recognize this.

She first met the brothers Copeland at the Grill when she was with her friend Meg. It was another insanely boring Christmastime in Delphi and the roommates had decided to get drunk on syrupy sloe gin fizzes. Philip offered to buy their drinks. The girls accepted and squeezed into the booth. It was transactional, a small price to pay. The twins were good-looking, but she was more attracted to Mark because he was quiet. He didn't press. It wasn't that he lacked confidence. The brothers were almost interchangeable in that regard. It was that he had no desire to brag. He let life come to him. He was comfortable in his own skin. It was an unusual quality in a college freshman. Kate decided she wanted to get to know him better.

When Kate was eleven years old her mother committed suicide by sleeping pill. Kate was unaware of the cause of death until she was fourteen. Until then she had thought her mother went to sleep one night and never woke up. "God wanted her up in

Heaven." That was what her father told her. And, for a time, she had no reason to doubt him. Freshman year in high school she learned the truth after a senior cheerleader pushed her out of the way, screaming bitchily "Kill yourself why don't you." Heartless, cackling, teen laughter reverberated off the steel lockers and hardwood hallways. It was a moment she would never forget.

Her father wanted to remove her from the school after the incident. Kate was adamant about staying. She chastised her father for lying until he apologized. They never discussed the matter again.

Smart people do the dumbest fucking things, thought Kate. She had just watched Mark and Philip heave their father's ashes high into a howling wind. What did they think would happen? She pulled her lavender scarf over her mouth to hide the smirk on her face. The gleaming brass vase dropped to the dirt with a thud. Mark laughed. Philip shouted. While the twins wiped off Walter's incinerated remains, Kate looked west across the lake and thought about her mother. Since the funeral, Kate had never once visited her mother's gravesite. She couldn't even remember if it had a headstone. Her mother had been dead half Kate's life. She wouldn't recognize her if she appeared between the parting clouds, like an angel, calling her name. All Kate had were a few fading memories. It had always been just her and Dad. The sun was high and bright and cold. Below, the wind pitched wave after wave against the rusty rocks. Her father, too, would be gone one day. No one gets younger. Things happen. And then she would be alone.

"I think you've got some right there," said Mark, flicking Philip's nose.

"Touch me again and I'll pummel you," said Philip.

Mark laughed again and hooked Kate's arm. Philip picked up the fallen urn. Joan replaced the lid and grinned.

There was opinionated discussion about the seating arrangements for the drive home. Philip offered to act as chauffeur. "Mark can sit in the passenger seat," he said, "and the women can sit in the back seat. That way they can avoid any ash."

"What about Dad?"

"We'll put him in the trunk. He's mostly gone with the wind anyway."

"I'll drive, thank you very much," said Joan. "I got us here without incident, didn't I?"

"Fine," said Philip. "It's Kate who has to suffer."

"Kate can sit in the front passenger seat. Philip, put your father in the trunk. I don't want to have to vacuum this car again. You boys sit in the rear. Problem solved."

No one spoke on the way back to Delphi. Kate hid her face in her scarf and looked out the side window at leafless trees and barren farm fields. There was nothing joyous about Iowa winters and there were times she didn't mind not having a mother.

For a nanosecond she was mortified. She had put her hand on Philip's genitals. She had made an awful error. She was stunned. She recoiled. Then she saw that he wasn't angry. She saw the look in his eyes. It was a familiar goatish look. She stood her ground. She stayed close. She teased him. She met his stare and imagined what it would be like to be with him. She wondered if he would be different from Mark. She wondered if she would be different with him. He acted cool and controlled but she could see his frogging pulse. His jaw slackened as he tried to regulate his breathing. He joked. He offered her coffee. She joked back. She flirted a bit. She fluttered her lashes and lowered her voice until it was a sexy whisper. It was harmless. They both liked it.

Joan extinguished the excitement, entering loudly with her omniscient smile. Philip poured his mother steaming coffee and the matriarch feigned a muddled apology. Something in her tone suggested deception, thought Kate. She concluded that Joan wasn't sorry about the mix up in the slightest. Kate stopped short, however, of believing the mistake was intentional. The woman had, after all, just lost her husband. She was entitled a little leeway. Still, she felt Joan was to blame for whatever happened. She blamed her for having identical twins. Ergo, she was to blame for any resulting confusion.

Mark kissed Kate on the shoulder. His wet black hair was cold on her cheek. He poured himself coffee and sat next to his mother.

"How'd everyone sleep?" he asked. "I found some of Dad's ashes on my pillow this morning. I have a feeling he's going to be around for a while."

Joan smiled.

Kate looked out the window. An airliner's contrails swelled and merged into one long fake cloud. She watched Philip finish his coffee. He placed his cup in the sink and left without a word. She wouldn't have let it go too far. Had he bent down to kiss her she would have slapped him. She was loyal to Mark. She was a good girlfriend. And good girlfriends do not cheat on good boyfriends.

Though, truth told, there was that one time, junior year. But it didn't count. Not to Kate. She considered it a technical violation. It was acting. It wasn't real. It was her role.

The story I heard goes something like this.

She and Meg had gone to the Phi Delta Tau party because it was Saturday night in Delphi and there was nothing better to do. The music was loud and the drinks were free. The frat house was hot and crowded, the floors sludgy. Kate lost Meg in the congestion and later when she found her alone on the front steps her friend was in tears.

"He called me a beat townie. Said he wouldn't waste a second on some skank who wasn't even doable when hammered," she cried.

"Who was it?"

Kate marched up the steps and back into the party. Her first instinct was to punch the bastard in the face right in front of all his yahoo frat brothers. She decided that was too good for him. She found her target in the kitchen playing quarters. Boozy cheers erupted after the coin's double clink. The air was heavy with belching and cheap cigar smoke. She maneuvered next to her prey, close. She let her thigh brush his arm. He looked up and gave her a sloppy smile. She put her hand on his shoulder. And she waited. When it was his turn she whispered in his ear, "Miss this, please. For me. I was hoping for a tour of your room." Her quarry dropped the quarter to the floor, announced "Game over!" and led her upstairs.

Kate and Meg had been friends for years, since the seventh grade. Meg was Kate's only girlfriend. Roommates every year in college, Kate would do anything to protect her friend. Townies stick together. No one hurts my Meg, Kate thought as she ascended the staircase.

He switched off the lights. Kate switched them back on. She licked her lips and placed his hands on her ass. She kissed him forcefully and grinded against him. She pushed him away and unbuttoned two buttons exposing her bra. She kissed him harder and rubbed his crotch with both hands. She pushed him away again.

"Your pants seem to be getting a little tight. Wouldn't you like to be more comfortable?"

He almost fell to the floor tripping out of his khakis. He stripped off his shirt. She moved in again and slid her tongue into his mouth while thrusting one hand deep inside his shorts.

"Come on. Show me what you've got. You're not shy, are you?"

He obeyed and dropped his underwear. The plaid boxers gathered around his ankles. She took a step back and put her hands on her hips. Then she burst into exaggerated laughter.

"You've got to be kidding me! What do you

expect me to do with that? Ha! Ha! And what is it anyway? If that's a dick it's the smallest one I've ever seen. Do us all a favor and keep whatever it is in your pants. Keep your nub to yourself."

She buttoned her blouse. He went limp. But she wasn't finished.

"Loser, I wouldn't waste a second of my time on that pathetic little thing."

She swung the door wide open. The silenced partiers in the corridor parted. Pointing, she walked away shouting over the music.

"Smallest penis in the world right in there! No admission charge! Absolutely free to the public! Hurry! See it while it you can!"

Kate never told Mark what she had done. There was no reason. It had nothing to do with him. It had nothing to do with their relationship. It was not a case of infidelity. It was a matter of loyalty.

Reared among the ubiquitous eyes, oversized ears and overworked mouths of a small farming town, she understood the importance of silos. Privacy in Delphi demanded forethought and grit. And without a private life you could never hope to escape. So Kate kept her lives, her personas, separate. By turns she was college student, townie, actress or girlfriend. She could be motherless, hard, caring, ambitious or needy. She could be beautiful or hideous. She could be all these but never at the same time, never fully exposed.

For that reason, and others, she wasn't thrilled when her father made Mark his assistant at the union. That they got along was even worse. Mark called her dad by his first name. She was embarrassed. Not of her father. She loved him as much as one can love. Rather, she was embarrassed in the way a six-year-old girl is embarrassed when she finds out, as most must, that she isn't a real princess. It's the disappointment of ordinariness. As a carefree coed she could pretend to be alone, without family and the concomitant mediocrity. She worked hard to forget that her dad worked a menial job at the small Midwestern college. And she avoided the union like the plague. When Mark announced his new job she tried to talk him out of it. It was a malignant blend. It was cancerous. It was one thing for her to pretend to be part of a professor's ideal family. It was quite another for Mark to pretend to be part of hers. It was backwards. It was going the wrong way.

The morning Philip left the brothers barely spoke. Waiting in the bus station was awkward for all the wrong reasons. It was not a happy farewell. Joan, noted Kate, appeared to be the only one at ease. The bus pulled away and Mark turned to his mother.

"I need to get some things. I'll see you in a little while."

Walking to his apartment, Mark told Kate about his argument with Philip and moving back home. Kate knew Mark wasn't angry about living with his mother. He was angry about the fight with his brother. He was tired of losing.

"He spoke to me like I was a child. He was dismissive. I don't need that shit in my life."

"I'm sure he didn't mean it."

In Kate's opinion they were both acting like

41

babies. But she wasn't about to get between twins. Their father just died, she thought, and they're manufacturing more drama. Perhaps fighting with your sibling is a coping mechanism. She was glad she was an only child.

Mark's apartment smelled like men and pizza. Kate wouldn't miss it. She helped him throw some things into suitcases and they fooled around a little. She wanted to make him forget his troubles. She felt he needed to forget. And she was a good girlfriend.

1990
LEFT LOBE
THE FOX

IN 1990, MY PARENTS were married in Northern California. The event is the centerpiece of act 2. I have their original marriage certificate here on my desk. Their faded signatures are flowing and youthful, full of hope. My father's calligraphy is bold. My mother's artistic. The ceremony was held high in the dotted, grape-growing hills of Napa Valley. I've since visited the vineyard and its chateau. (At one point I even considered buying the estate as a memento and sanctuary.) It's an exceptional site. And when I was younger, according to my mother, I would spend hours in front of the television— thick monocle strapped to my angled head—watching the nuptials over and over and over again. I no longer remember why I found the video so captivating. Perhaps its two-dimensions appealed to my lack of depth perception. Then again

43

maybe I was attracted to the dazzling contrasts: the blacks and whites of elegant suits and frilly dresses, the bright green grass and the deep blue sky. It was a lot like watching a cartoon in Technicolor. I remember there was a blue and white hot air balloon. There was music and singing and dancing and drinking, long white-clothed tables peppered with glinting plates and thin-stemmed glasses ruby red with wine. The people were strangers but not, like serial television actors. I still have the old VHS tape. I keep it in a special banker's box along with my other memories. I haven't viewed the cassette in years. I'd watch it now but I've misplaced my VHS player. Forgive me, I've rambled enough about an old video. Back to the story. My mother takes the stage first.

KATE

Kate remained in Delphi for more than a year after commencement. She and Mark lived like blithe college students without the nuisance of classes or coursework. Mark lived with his mother. Kate lived with her father. Their expenses were negligible. Mark made more than enough working days at the student union and Kate's father still provided a small weekly allowance. They spent their nights at the Grill in conversation, already reminiscing about their university days and forever dreaming of their futures. On Friday or Saturday nights they sometimes made it up to Des Moines for dinner or a concert or a club. Kate expected Mark to do something with his life. She waited. She hoped he would do something. He talked about graduate school. He talked about moving to New York, writing a book, traveling the world. He talked about a lot of things. But he did nothing. He stayed put. He seemed, to Kate, happy to be where he was. He appeared happy in Delphi. Kate was not. Life in Iowa was not enough. She had given him a year. And that was enough. She made plans to leave.

In 1986, with her theater degree from Wallace and the promise of youth, Kate headed west to Hollywood in the graduation present from her father, a used 1982 Honda Civic, white and practical. The car was stuffed with her belongings, Mark among them. Mark went to California to keep her company and to spend an extra few days with her. Philip, who hadn't been back since Walter's death, flew to Iowa so Joan would not be alone. Still feuding, the brothers had no reason to meet.

On the way to California the couple detoured to the Grand Canyon. It was the first time either one of them had ever been there. It was a million times bigger and more colorful than the stunted bluffs at Red Rock, thought Kate. Mark was awestruck. She took a photo of him pretending to fall into a crevasse. They hiked to the canyon floor passing burros and floppy-hatted seniors with walking sticks. It was a wonderful trip. They took their time. They cruised on highways through the warm summer air with the windows down and the music loud. For long stretches, wherever they could, they left the soulless interstate and took old Route 66 to eat greasy food at dying diners, stop at kitschy souvenir stands and make the trip last a little bit longer.

Southern California was broad boulevards and

towering palms. Everything sparkled in the sunlight. Kate suspected her dirty white Honda and its Iowa plates stood out among the spotless, expensive autos of Los Angeles County. Wedged among gleaming convertibles they sailed the smooth suburban streets. It took them hours to reach the journey's end even though they had a good map and their destination was in the heart of Reseda, conveniently next to the freeway. Her communications professor at Wallace had set her up in an apartment with two former students. They were actors too, older actors, Scott and Lisa. They were in their thirties. They had been in California for years.

Kate was more excited than afraid. Mark helped her unload her belongings. Scott and Lisa seemed nice, very laid back, very chill. Kate's bedroom was small and windowless, but it was enough. It was hers.

Mark stayed with her in the tiny bedroom for a few days until she could get settled. Map in hand they played tourist, visiting strange sites. They investigated the La Brea tar pits. They went up to Griffith Observatory where Kate pretended to be Natalie Wood. They drove past the big movie studios' over-sized gates. At a used clothing store on Melrose, Mark bought a London Fog plaid trench coat for five dollars. They had long lunches in cheap restaurants, Mark reading aloud the latest list of open calls in *Backstage*.

She dropped him off at LAX without going inside the terminal. Parking would have been a hassle and a needless waste of money. They kissed by the curb.

Mark gave her his copy of *One Hundred Years of Solitude*. Tears blurred their vision. The good-bye was brief. Kate got stuck in traffic on the way back to Reseda. She wondered if she'd made a huge mistake.

Right away—on her second audition after three call backs—she landed a chewing gum commercial. It wasn't a speaking part. All she had to do was smile. She was good at smiling. She was pretty. She was youthful. In post-production they made one tooth twinkle. She was on her way. Her roommates were indifferent. They were jaded and hadn't worked in months. They lived off their dwindling savings and Kate's rent. They told Kate they'd probably have to move if things didn't pick up.

At first she spoke with Mark every night, captivating conversations that lasted late, then the calls became every few days, then every week and finally, unceremoniously, they both decided the long distance relationship thing wasn't really working. "You will always be my first love," they each had said. Kate cried for a day and then got another call back. She began to meet people and explore her neighborhood. She concentrated on her new life. Every once in a while she received a letter or phone call from Joan. They would talk as friends. Joan would sound worried. Kate would ask about Mark.

It would be more than a year before she got a second acting gig. She had resorted to waitressing at a local pizzeria to make ends meet. Gas, rent, utilities, food, there never seemed to be enough money. California was expensive. Her dad helped her out whenever he could.

She had one line in her second commercial. The ad was for a malodorous male deodorant. The hirsute, foul-smelling lead actor supposedly smells wonderfully masculine and fresh once he applies a few swipes of the miracle balm. Kate sidles up to him and says, 'Smells like you're about to get lucky.' It was an awful advertisement. But it was work. During casting she had worried she wouldn't get the role. After the second call back she slept with the director on the promise that it would earn her the part. It did. She was desperate for the work.

My mother once told me—I was a teenager at the time—that should she ever write her memoirs she would emphasize that she felt more defiled playing a slut in that dreadful commercial than sleeping with the opportunistic director. Later, in fact, she hired a private investigator to locate and acquire every existing hardcopy of that ad. She threw them into the fireplace and watched them burn.

By the end of 1988 Kate had had enough. She had expected express stardom. She thought beauty and talent and resolve were the only ingredients needed for Hollywood success. It did not go as planned. She had miscalculated or been naive. She grew tired of the relentless sun and the constant traffic. She despised Reseda. She had few friends. Her Honda was showing its age. She had done two commercials in two and a half years. (And she had to sleep with the director to get one of them.) She was always low on money, always scrimping. Over a bad dinner a lousy agent told her there was always decent money in adult films. Scott and Lisa raised her rent every three months. Her dad sent another check. He wrote that it would have to be the last for a spell. Her life was heading in the wrong direction. So Kate decided acting was not her future. Neither, to be sure, was waitressing. She didn't know what to do next. She didn't want to return to Iowa but she didn't know where to turn, where to focus her energy.

Joan tried to help. She asked Kate whether she needed money. Kate declined politely. An hour after she spoke to Joan, Mark telephoned and offered to come out west and take her back to Delphi. That was the last thing she needed. They hadn't spoken in almost two years and he wanted to ride to her aid as if they'd never separated. He begged. He used every tool in the shed. "Your dad misses you. My mom misses you. I miss you. Meg. You belong here. This is your home. The Grill isn't the same. Nothing's the same. Come on, please. Remember our trip? Remember how much fun we had? It'll be like that but in reverse. Remember how happy we were? It can be that way again. Don't you remember how in love we were?" Kate lost track of how many times she said no. He went on and on. She didn't want to be unkind but he was hurting her.

"Mark, we're done. I'm never coming back to Delphi. I am sorry. I have to go. Good-bye."

A few days later Kate answered a loud rap on the door. She looked through the security hole and saw Mark standing there grinning from ear to ear. She threw the door open and screamed.

"I told you, Mark. It's over."

"Kate, I'm—"

"Oh, Philip, it's you. I'm sorry. I thought you were your brother."

MARK

In a black notebook stuffed with gasoline receipts, pressed leaves and beer bottle labels, Mark describes the drive to California as 'the best and worst trip any young man head over heels in love can ever take.' He goes on to catalogue the various stops, the people and places, waitresses and way stations, panhandlers and panhandles, cattle and cacti, but mostly he records the conversations with Kate. And they are wet with melancholy. Whether debating picking up a hitchhiker or deciding where to stop for lunch, they are all sad, plaintive; as if he knew whatever they had together was coming to an end—nostalgia of the present.

There's a picture of them standing on an unremarkable street corner in Arizona. I found it years ago in a shoebox full of faded photographs. It's my favorite photo of them as a couple. It captures their era, their essence, their youth. Mark stands straight and tall with a broad knowing grin. Kate is laughing, head tilted, one foot off the ground leaning in close to Mark. It almost appears as if she was in the middle of a fall and Mark had saved her, one handed. They look happy, like in a movie, a beautiful young couple on a big western adventure, clinging to each other in the setting sun. On the back of the photo it says, '1986 – Standing on a corner in Winslow, Arizona. Ha. Ha'. I have no idea what's so funny. My mother smiles and says it's from an old song.

Southern California has a distinctive smell, thought

Mark, sweet and fecund. It is a place for births, not deaths, beginnings, not endings. It's intoxicating. He could taste the air. He knew immediately it was all too much, that Los Angeles was a place to explore and visit, to appreciate and leave. It is a vacation destination. But it's too cloying, too warm and comfortable, for living. Kate loved it. She bubbled with excitement. She loved everything about it. She even adored her hideous, windowless bedroom in bland, neglected, noisy Reseda. Mark was jealous and afraid. He made jokes about sharks and sunstroke, earthquakes and brush fires.

He should have left as soon as possible but didn't. He lingered for a few days and drove around with Kate pretending everything was fine. He knew the relationship was over. He knew he couldn't—and wouldn't—compete. On Hollywood Boulevard he discovered his hands matched Clint Eastwood's. One afternoon, while Kate met industry people with her new roommates, he attempted to make his way up to the Hollywood sign. He walked through alien suburbs, house after house, black street numbers stenciled on tall clean curbs. The driveways featured large unattended boxes of avocadoes. Homemade signs announced: 'Avocadoes, Five for a Quarter.' Not a homeowner, not another living person, in sight. All based on the honor system. Even coming from small town Iowa, Mark knew something about it wasn't right. Discouraged and bored, he changed his mind and went back to Reseda to wait for Kate. He never made it up to the giant sign on the hillside. It didn't matter.

Mark was away from Joan for two weeks. When he returned Philip was gone. He heard all about him though.

"Philip's business is really taking off, Mark," she said. "Quite extraordinary, I don't understand what it is but it's a tremendous success and something computer people desperately need. He adores California. He shares a place with his business associates. It sounds like a fraternity house. It was lovely having him here, seeing him again. I wish we all could have been together. That would have been nice, I suppose."

"I suppose."

"You know, at the end, I was all by myself for almost three whole days. It was odd." She paused. "But before he left Phillip made sure I had everything I needed. Oh, and Mr. Purcell stopped by. We had coffee. We talked about you and Kate. I asked him how the union was doing. He is a very kind man. He's worried about his daughter, and rightfully so, one should think."

His mother's mention of Mr. Purcell reminded Mark that he had an early start in the morning. He kissed her twice, told her it was nice to be home and went up to bed. He fell asleep trying to recall California's peculiar fragrance.

He had promised to phone Kate every night and for a while he kept the promise. He made his days in Delphi seem more exciting than they actually were and he assumed she was doing the same for Reseda. More often than not she wasn't around when he called. The calls became shorter and fewer. And, one day, they called it quits. Mark was hurt but he had gotten used to being alone. He had seen it coming.

Though he had worked to make Delphi sound more interesting for Kate's benefit, the truth—his truth, at least—was that it was plenty interesting. He was more than content. He spent his days working for Mr. Purcell, Chuck, at the union among the students, staff and faculty. After the split, Chuck didn't mention Kate, but they got along all the same. They worked well together. The union was the hub of the college. Students went there to check their mail, grab a bite, and, often, quiz Mark about a certain professor or assignment. He never tired of their stressed-out stories: the impossible exam, the late term paper, the low grade because of an unfair curve. Nights were spent with Earl at the Grill, sipping coffee, maybe enjoying a beer or two. Sometimes he'd play pool with coeds. And he took care of his mother. He made sure she kept busy and had everything she wanted. On weekends and lunch breaks, weather permitting and sometimes not, he'd go for long quiet walks and absorb everything he could. He held his tongue out to the rain and rubbed the soil between his fingers. He whistled with the birds and barked at the dogs. He did what he told his father he was going to do. He lived.

At some point Mark began to write down his thoughts in increasing detail. It helped him refine his reasoning. It kept him on track. He had always kept a journal, always taken notes on life, but now he started to sculpt these disparate, congealing thoughts and impressions into mini narratives. Like everything he did, he did it for himself. Still, it's likely that his literary career began as a way to compete with the stories of his brother's accumulating success or maybe he thought his dad would approve. It didn't matter why it began. It became part of his life, like the long solo walks, like the job at the union, like caring for his mother.

The structural idea for his first efforts came from the back brick wall of the Grill. As a promotion, Earl offered patrons the opportunity to buy a brick. For ten dollars they could have whatever they wanted engraved—assuming it was decent, of course—on the brick of their choice, plus they'd get a foamy pitcher of beer in the bargain. There weren't many open spots left. The wall was packed with two-and-a-quarter-by-eight-inch rectangles proclaiming eternal love or eternal friendship or eternal fidelity. "Eternal silliness," Earl said. 'Billy loves Sally' was one. 'Phi Delts Rule!' was another, complete with fat Greek letters and the class of 1977 membership list. Some were more cryptic, like the one that read, 'Hey, you, yeah you, the one reading me, you owe me a drink.' Some were philosophical, 'You are a shadow and do not exist.' All were personal and public. All were pleas. Night after night Mark stared at the long red wall listening to Earl. All those bricks, all those stories. It was like they spoke to him.

The first story he finished, the only one he felt was complete, made the rounds at Wallace in samizdat fashion. An English professor told Mark he ought to send it to the *Atlantic*. He did and they liked it. The November 1988 issue hit the stands with "Chipped Away" by Mark E. Copeland on page eighteen. A poem by Nobel Prize winner Czeslaw Milosz appeared on the same page. Mark was proud and self-conscious in equal parts. The day it came out he purchased a copy at the union; he sniffed it, rolled it up like a baton and went for a long, long walk.

At the house his mother told him to call Kate. "She isn't doing well. I don't think it's working out for her." Mark called and offered to bring her back home. She dismissed him. He didn't bother telling her about his story.

PHILIP

In 1984, when he was in his final year at Caltech, the same year his father was killed, two articles appeared in the press that would change Philip's life. The first was a little read piece warning about the then novel concept of computer viruses. Few at the time took the threat seriously. But Philip had looked into the eye of the future and was confident he was to be the industry's Jonas Salk. The second article was in *Time* magazine. Bill Gates was featured on the cover. Personal computing had hit the big time. It had gone mainstream. So after graduation Philip and another classmate, Jeb, moved up to Northern California into a little, rented house in Sunnyvale with a Stanford drop-out. Two years later they founded a company they named Aegis. Aegis was the first commercial anti-virus program and Philip was its creator and CEO. Even before they had formed an official partnership, before they'd sold a single unit, investors were begging them to take their money. No one wanted to miss the next big thing. No one wanted to miss out on the next Microsoft. Philip was the right man in the right place at the right time.

I have a maroon scrapbook my grandmother gave me when I was twelve; its leatherette cover is now webbed with cracks. The album contains photos and newspaper articles about Philip and Mark. One clipping is an interview with Philip from 1987, the year Aegis was incorporated. The bold headline warns "Your Computer is Coughing." Reading the article you get the sense the reporter asking the questions doesn't really understand or believe in the notion of a computer virus. At one point he asks Philip: 'Can I catch one of these viruses standing here talking to you?' Philip replies drily: 'Not yet, technology isn't that advanced. One day, in the not too distant future, though, you will be at risk. Yes.' Philip was solemn. You can almost see the reporter roll his eyes. Still, the piece is mostly flattering. The paper is now yellowing. The print is dull. There's a handwritten note in blue ink at the bottom: 'For Mom.'

Philip was twenty-five and rich. He sent money home and asked his mother to make sure Mark had enough, though she was under order not to explain its origins. Philip was rich but his lifestyle hadn't changed. Other companies materialized, copying his concept, mimicking his code. And, because Aegis was the first to market, every geek miscreant in the civilized world was trying to circumvent its defenses. He lived in the same small house in Sunnyvale. (His roommates took their new-found money and moved to more spacious accommodations.) He coded. He battled. He lived at the keyboard, alone. And he was happy. There was always another challenge, another problem to be solved. He had no time for anything else. He wanted nothing else. He was driven by his ideas, by his skill and by his vision of the future.

Every so often, however, the non-stop programming, the constant need to evolve, the unending requirements, all got to be too much. When this happened, when Philip felt it reaching critical mass, he called a travel agent and escaped for a week or two, usually to some secluded locale, quiet, technologically primitive. He was packing for Fiji when his mother telephoned.

"I know you're about to go on your big trip to the deserted island, but would you do me a favor beforehand."

"Of course."

"On your way would you stop in and see Kate Purcell in Los Angeles. She's not doing well, the poor dear. I'm worried about her. She's all alone. I promised her father we would look in on her. And, Philip, be nice."

Philip scribbled Kate's address on the note pad he always carried. He vowed never to give his mother his itinerary again.

"Don't worry, I'll be nice, Mom."

When he was a boy Philip despised being mistaken for his brother. It was the bane of his childhood. Just the idea that anyone could think he was Mark infuriated him to the point of rage. Maybe that's why he felt he needed to leave Iowa. Maybe he needed to be far away from his brother to be himself. Kate Purcell was the last person to make the mistake and that had been four years ago in Iowa. She did it a second time the instant she opened her apartment door.

"I told you, Mark. It's over."

"Kate, I'm—"

As soon as he spoke she apologized. Glints of the Copeland kitchen incident danced in their eyes.

"What are you doing here? Oh, my manners. Come in, please."

He explained that his mother had made him come.

"Apparently everyone is worried about you."

"That's just silly," she said. "I'm fine, as you can see. Can I get you something to drink?"

"Sure, if you have a beer, I'll take one. But I can't stay long."

He sat on a slouching couch and watched her shear the caps off two green beer bottles. This place is a dump, he thought. He wondered how long he'd have to stay to 'be nice.'

By his third beer Philip forgot about Fiji. He wasn't used to alcohol and he was having a wonderful time. He asked Kate if she was hungry. He was hungry. They locked up the apartment—an apartment that contained nothing worth stealing—and walked up an unattractive avenue around a corner and into a dingy Mexican restaurant. Philip ordered steak enchiladas. Kate got a chicken burrito. The meal's first half was spent talking about Mark. Kate had raised the topic.

"You probably know more about him than I do," said Philip. I haven't seen him in years. We barely speak. We haven't been close."

"I think the last time we talked I wasn't very nice. I hope he's happy."

They imagined Mark at the Grill sitting on an uneven stool, legs crossed, staring into space, Earl rinsing glasses in the background.

"How can he stand those awful Iowa winters?"

Philip told her about the story in the *Atlantic*.

"It's quite well done, though I'm no critic."

"Good for him. I'm glad he did something. Oh, Christ, I hope he didn't write about me," said Kate.

"I don't think so, unless you're German. It's about two former lovers, Berliners, separated the night the Berlin Wall was built and reunited on the night it comes down thirty years later. At the end they realize too much time has passed. Their love was weaker than the wall."

"Sounds sad. What does he know about Germany? He's never been out of the country."

"I don't know. He reads a lot."

Kate entertained Philip with the indignities faced by a struggling young actress in Los Angeles. She kept it light, farcical, not tragic, not pathetic. She explained the filming process and its crusade for perfection, its endless number of takes and retakes, its repetition.

"It sounds like programming," he said.

"Programming can't be that boring. It's all waiting around for a few seconds of camera, action, life. It's mind numbing mostly."

Kate asked about Joan.

"She's fine. Mark takes care of her. I'll deny if asked, but I think they like sharing a house. They'll probably be together forever."

"Your mother has been very sweet to me."

They recalled the last time they'd seen each other. After the funeral. Kate said that Walter was a good man. They both agreed he was missed. They ordered more beer. They laughed about the ash ceremony.

"You were so angry," said Kate. "You didn't see the humor in it then."

"I do now. And that's what counts."

Kate tried to replicate Philip's angry, ashed face but failed. They were both laughing too hard.

Kate talked about how much she worried about her dad. Philip said he was nice to check in on his mom. "Widow and widower looking out for each other," he said. Kate changed the subject by telling Philip Meg was still in Delphi but married with children. Philip couldn't place the name.

"You don't remember Meg? Then you don't remember the first time we met? I am officially offended. For that you owe me another beer," said Kate stripping the label off her almost empty bottle.

JOAN

Joan had arranged it so Philip would arrive just after Mark left for the coast with Kate. She didn't want to be alone any longer than she had too, nor was she taking any chances on the boys meeting. She scheduled a two week vacation from the office. Philip arrived with a weary preoccupied look. He told her it had been a long trip and his head was still filled with work. It had been almost two years since she had seen her eldest son. He's turning into such a man, she thought. He—they—look a lot like Walter.

After a day or two under Joan's care, Philip relaxed and enjoyed his mother's pampering. Joan buttered his morning toast and changed his pressed sheets. He took her shopping and they watched television or played Scrabble together. They talked about everything and anything. She wanted to hear all about California and the business. In the early evenings Philip walked around Delphi, alone, like his brother, visiting former haunts. He even stopped by the Grill and said hello to Earl.

"He sends his best," Philip said. "Not much changes around here, does it?"

Toward the end of his stay Joan asked him if he wanted to go out to the cliffs at Lake Red Rock, now renamed Walter's Bluff by the Copelands.

"It's beautiful up there this time of year," she said. "Mark and I go all the time. We like to talk to your father."

"If you want to go, I'll go."

"I was thinking about you, Philip."

"If it's all the same, I'd rather stay here."

Philip apologized for having to leave earlier than expected. Work called. It couldn't be helped.

"And Mark will be back in a couple of days," he said.

Joan did everything she could to get him to stay. She even resorted to faking a minor illness. Philip promptly called a doctor and the ruse failed. The doctor, packing up his little black bag, said it was probably psychosomatic.

"Nothing to be concerned about. Nerves is all. Your mother's in fine fettle," he reported.

Pronounced cured, Joan washed and ironed Philip's once-worn clothes and helped him repack. She told him she would miss him. She told him to be careful out there in California, to call whenever he could, not to work too hard. She told him she hoped it wouldn't be two years before they saw each other again.

Joan waved good-bye with both arms as Philip drove away in the shiny red rental car. It started to drizzle. She worried about his drive up to Des Moines. The roads are winding. She wanted to tell him to be careful. The pavement would be slippery. But he was already halfway down the block. She sighed and went inside. On the kitchen counter she found an envelope containing a check.

Joan and Mark lived in the same house, night and day, and thus had a very different dynamic. Mark had his life. Joan had hers. They lived their separate lives, together. They rarely watched television with each other. And they never played Scrabble. Mark was self-sufficient. He wouldn't let Joan do the smallest chore if he could help it. He did his own laundry and cooked most meals. True, they visited Walter's Bluff once a month. It had become a ritual. She suspected

Mark may have gone more often—without her—but she never pried. That was his business. They didn't talk much. So Joan didn't bother telling Mark she still spoke with Kate after the breakup. It would have been a breach. Mother and second son didn't communicate in such an overt way.

I once asked Joan—this was, it must be said, many, many years after the fact—why she had remained in touch with my mother after her breakup with Mark. Shouldn't she have sided with her son? Had she ever thought she was being disloyal? And she told me, 'I stayed friendly with Kate all those years because I liked her. She had been a part of our family. Well, that and the fact she lost her mother, the poor, poor thing. She needed a mother. And her father had always been nice to us. I never had a daughter, until Kate. She reminded me of myself maybe. That's a lot, isn't it? It would have been a lot to let go of. Anyway, it seemed that way at the time.'

Joan, in fact, first learned about the separation from Kate, not Mark. Kate had cried during the call. She felt awful and said it was all her fault. Joan told her not to trouble herself. "These things happen," she said, "no one is to blame." Mark, on his own, later confessed they were no longer a couple. He said flatly, "all promises in life and love are one day broken." And he told her he had nothing more to say on the subject. Joan believed he was hiding his hurt for her sake. She didn't know how to get him to open up without the possibility she'd upset him, so she didn't try.

She worried about her boys. Sometimes, late at night, she thought her worry was the only thing keeping her going. She wished they could all be together again, like it had been before Walter's accident. Life had been almost perfect. Whenever she longed this way the amplified warning soon followed. '*One son will be the death of the other.*' She couldn't take the risk.

Joan wondered what Walter would say about her scheming. To be sure, he would call her foolish. He would laugh. He would most likely remind her that behind the painted papier mâché rocks were twittering graduate students, not inspired prophets. What they said was gibberish, not ghoulish. It was done for fun. Our boys will be just fine. But Walter was no longer around to challenge her. His voice had been silenced. She was alone and alive and hers was the only perspective that mattered. Still, she would have liked to hear him say she was doing the right thing; she would have liked some validation.

One afternoon Mr. Purcell—he was emphatic she call him Chuck—stopped by to say hi and have a quick cup of coffee. Mark was manning the student union on his own. As they usually did they talked about their children. Kate was having real difficulties. She was questioning her dream of becoming a famous actress, Chuck had said. She disliked Los Angeles. He hoped she would come back to Delphi. But he was afraid to tell her because it might backfire. He didn't know what to do. He couldn't send her any more money. Joan felt embarrassed, almost guilty. Her children were doing so well. Philip's business was booming and Mark had published his story. She wanted to say something reassuring. She wanted to impart some bit of maternal wisdom, but everything she thought of sounded like a platitude. She didn't know how to make him feel better. For a second she considered telling him about her premonitory need to keep the twins apart. Such a crazy confession might ease his anxieties. Appearances to the contrary, we all have our issues, it would have said. And it would have been good to share the burden with someone, someone kind. A vulpine grin parted her lips. She hesitated. She wasn't worried that he'd think she was deranged; she was worried he'd think she was mean. She lipped her cup. Chuck changed the subject to the new psychology professor's penchant for morning crullers. The window had shut. She kept the secret to herself.

Kate called and repeated what her father had said. Joan offered to help. Kate said she didn't know what kind of help she needed or wanted. Joan broke protocol and told Mark. He called her but Kate didn't want his help. Two days later Joan called Philip and asked him to give it a try.

KATE

It was a whirlwind. One minute she had next to nothing and, then, she had everything. Philip knocked, they talked and he asked her out to dinner. The meal lasted a week. Philip canceled his travel plans and had his bags brought to homely Reseda. Kate ditched work. They spent hours rolling around on her mattress in the windowless bedroom. They showered and ate together. Then they went back to the bedroom for more. At the end of the week Philip asked her to move in with him. She said yes and packed. Philip left a generous check for Scott and Lisa before heading north to Sunnyvale. Kate welcomed the change. She played house. She took care of her new man and her new life without the worry of a budget. She had something to do. She felt she could breathe again. She felt alive. Within six months Philip dropped to one knee and asked Kate to marry him and without hesitation she said yes.

In the purblind excitement of new love she hadn't given much thought to Mark. Neither had Philip, she suspected. At the beginning they both questioned if they were doing something wrong; but, upon admittedly passionate reflection, they concluded they were not. Mark didn't own her. He had no claim. Kate rationalized that her prior misidentifications— the Copeland kitchen, the apartment door—were not mistakes at all. They were omens, signs. It had always been Philip. Yes, she had been in love with Mark, but it had been a first love, a puppy love, practice. Mark wasn't the man for her. Mark wasn't the marrying, have-a-picket-fence-and-a-family type. Mark wasn't practical. He wasn't mature. Yes, she had been in love. Mark was wonderful. And, yes, she had thought about being his wife. But in her heart, despite the fun and the fantasy, she knew it would never work. They were too different. Mark had been a stepping stone. She needed more. She needed a better foundation. She needed a stability Mark could never provide. Philip was her next step. He was the rock she required. She remembered Meg had once told her,

"You don't marry someone for their potential." Mark would always have potential. Philip's potential had been realized. And that made all the difference.

An investor in Aegis owned a winery in Napa and offered the estate to Philip for the wedding. The property hugged a hillside overlooking the valley. Its broad green lawn, brightly lit beneath sun-purpled mountains, was flanked by ripening grapevines. The setting was magical. Before she could become Mrs. Philip Edward Copeland, though, there was work to be done.

Philip told her not to worry about money and she didn't. Three hundred guests were invited. Meg was to be Kate's maid of honor. Jeb, Philip's business partner, was his best man. Kate and Philip spent hours discussing the arrangements. They agreed on most everything. Philip wanted her to have whatever she wanted. Money smoothed most wrinkles. But they spent a lot of time debating Mark's invitation. Neither one wanted to make it any worse. They wanted to be sensitive to his feelings. In the end they sent him an invitation. Mark replied promptly that he would not be attending but wished the happy couple a lifetime of happiness.

Kate arranged first class airline tickets for her father and Joan. They sat in seats 1A and 1B on the flight west. Kate had a car meet them at SFO and chauffeur them to the hotel. It was the first time she'd seen either of them in four years. Her father cried. Joan gave her a big hug.

Nothing could possibly go wrong on such a beautiful day, thought Kate looking out the window of her suite. Not too hot, not too cold. A day meant to be. The yellow sun climbed a ladder of popcorn clouds. The lawn and the bunting glistened. She could see guests gathering. She was nervous but in control. Meg and the other bridesmaids—girlfriends and wives of Philip's colleagues, her recently acquired new best friends—helped her prepare. They assured her that she was the most beautiful bride they had ever seen. She felt like a princess.

Having viewed the video a thousand times, I can easily bring it to my mind's eye. It really was almost perfect. And yet there was one thing out of place, one dissonance, in the almost perfect wedding: and it is my mother's frozen face. It doesn't fit. She was wearing what I have come to call 'the beautiful scowl.' I once asked her what she was thinking as she walked up the aisle, because—as I so tactlessly said as an adolescent—you look sad and stern, almost angry. You're dressed like a bride, you're beautiful, but you don't look happy. *She laughed and said, 'I was very nervous. It was a big occasion. The biggest. This was my life. I saw my future and maybe I just forgot how to act. Maybe the stage was too big for me. I don't know. It was so long ago. This is what I remember: The string quartet begins and everyone stands. My dad, your grandfather, tells me he loves me. I tell him not to make me cry; it'll ruin my makeup. I emerge from the chateau and pass under a trellis of flowers. My veil catches on something briefly. I see all those people, staring. I want to make sure they all get a good look so I walk down the endless aisle swiveling my head making eye contact with everyone I can. I don't want to miss anybody important. My dad is holding me too tightly—which made it*

68

difficult in that dress and those shoes to walk—and he has this stupid grin on his face. He couldn't be happier. I wonder whether he is thinking about his wife, my mom. Is he wishing she was here? I reckon he is just happy in the moment, happy for me. The aisle is long and lined with lilies. Little girls I don't know drop rose petals on the white carpet before me. They weave and stop at random. I finally reach the makeshift altar. I see Joan, your grandmother. She seems preoccupied. She doesn't share my father's happiness. It is like she is worrying about something. I assume she is thinking about Mark, which makes me think about Mark too. A part of me will always love him, I tell myself. But I am doing nothing wrong. I have to live my life my way. I try to shake the thought of Mark out of my head and then I see Philip. He is beaming, tall and proud. He is standing there, immaculate, waiting for me. And every other thought vanishes. My father disappears and the preacher starts talking but I can't take my eyes off Philip. A roar breaks the spell. Everyone looks toward the sound. Off to one side sits the hot air balloon, 'just married' streamers dangling from the tethered basket. After the ceremony the plan is to sail off into the sunset. The pilot has to occasionally release hot air to keep the balloon inflated and ready. The flame's roar is louder than I thought it would be. The pilot waves an apology. I shrug toward the audience and look again into Philip's blue eyes. He isn't disturbed in the slightest. I worry the noise will repeat and spoil the ceremony. No one will be able to hear the music. No one will hear our vows. And I want everyone there to hear me say 'I do.' That's what I was thinking about. That's what I remember. The pained look on my face is probably the reason I never made it as an actor.'

MARK

As the marginally younger brother, Mark had always been treated as the baby in the family. Someone had to assume the role and he had been elected. It was a part he increasingly resented. He hated being patronized. It was his one true soft spot. A superior man will always be rankled by the condescending sympathy of inferiors. And, above all else, in whatever convoluted and immodest way, Mark considered himself superior. It was his essence. He believed his conspicuous quest for a simple lifestyle belied its— and his—genius. He thought few understood this or him.

When Philip and Kate became a couple the pity was oppressive, when they got engaged it became deafening and maddening. Mark was convinced Philip was largely to blame. It was another way to turn the screws. It appeared the rift between the brothers was permanent. But in truth Mark wasn't angry. He wasn't even jealous. He had loved Kate. And when it was over he moved on. It is what his philosophy demanded. No, he wasn't angry or jealous. But he was too perceptive and too sensitive not to admit there was probably part of him that should be. He spent months overanalyzing his feelings or the lack thereof. He raked through his past. He reread Romantic poets.

In early spring 1990 he writes, 'Love's stain remains long after love's object has gone. It is a reminder of one's ability to love. To scour or veil the past would be to dim one's own radiance.'

Mark's invitation to the wedding arrived before his mother's. It was cream-colored, heavy and expensive-looking. He tossed it aside.

"You're going to respond, aren't you?" she said. "You're not going to throw it in the garbage?"

"No, Mom, I'm not going to throw it away."

He told her he probably wasn't going to attend. He didn't think his presence would be appropriate. He felt it would be awkward for everyone. Joan quickly agreed and hinted that perhaps he should talk to a professional, maybe the pastor. She said it was perfectly acceptable to feel anger toward Philip. It was natural. "The main thing is not to turn your anger inward," she said. "Don't bottle it up." Her advice sounded to Mark like something she'd heard on daytime television. For weeks she kept returning to the same conversation, the same concerns. At times he wanted to scream, but he was well aware any sign of emotion would be taken as confirmation of his inner torment. He told her he was fine, really. "You go and have a good time. Don't worry about me. I'll send a gift."

Chuck handed Mark the keys to the student union.

"I know we never talked about things. It didn't seem right to. And I'm not the meddling kind. But, for the record, I'm sorry the way it worked out. I always pictured it being you and Kate."

Mark put the keys in his front pocket.

"It's okay. We both want what's best for Kate. Some things are meant to be and some aren't," said Mark.

"You're a good man. You deserve a good woman. Ah, but you're too young. Someday you'll find her. See you on Wednesday. Any troubles call at the hotel. And don't forget Monday's delivery."

Mark flipped the deadbolt and sat in the nearest chair. He scanned the union diner tapping his fingers on the table. He considered ways to improve business. The low countertop glistened drying. The napkin dispensers atop the refrigerator stood at attention like thickset aluminum soldiers. The potato chip rack was hidden, turned sideways. It should be up front, he thought. And the pretzel machine took up too much space. He'd get rid of it. He imagined rearranging the tables and chairs, creating a new pattern, one facing outward toward the leafy quad. The old cash register was in the wrong place. But it couldn't be moved, at least not without Chuck's approval and assistance. The color too was wrong. Instead of yellow, the walls should be in the school's colors, blue and white. If he was in charge he'd change the menu, expand it to include fresh items, made daily. While he was thinking about what kind of sandwiches to add to the menu he wondered whether he'd been selfish in declining their invitation to the wedding. Maybe he was being a little petulant after all. They *had* invited him. They wanted him there. He could still go. He could change his mind. He thought about calling to book a ticket. He could still make it in time. Chuck and his mother hadn't left yet. He could surprise them. Boy, wouldn't my appearance shock them all? He rose. The keys jingled in his pocket. He looked down at a scuff on the linoleum and had second thoughts. No, he had told them he wasn't coming. He decided to mop the floor instead.

The night before the big wedding—the notebook entry is dated—Mark, most likely in bed filling his journal with the day's events before falling asleep, writes, 'I remember Dad, in an undoubtedly fruitless and misplaced effort to explain the bygone workings of the ancient mind, once told me the legend of the Greek boy and the fox. The details have unfortunately disappeared from my memory, but the tale as I recall it involves a Spartan boy who steals a prize fox from his kindly neighbor. As he's making his escape he hears the neighbor approaching and hides the stolen fox in his shirt. Confronted and questioned about the crime he allows the hidden fox to bite his vitals rather than admit to the theft. On the eve of my brother's wedding this story says something about me and Philip and Kate, though I know not who plays the boy, who plays the fox or who plays the neighbor.'

Saturday it rained. The student union diner served up three meals for lunch: one number two: the hotdog special, which comes with ridged chips and a drink; and two number ones: the hamburger plate, a quarter pound patty, which comes with a generous side order of cheese fries. Mark sent the cook home early and thumbed through the *Enchiridion*. He closed the union early and tramped through the rain to the Grill. The drops felt good against his skin. He tried to estimate how many more times in this life he would walk through a warm driving rain. One thousand? One hundred? Fewer? More? He did his best to sear the sensation into his memory.

Earl was behind the bar. There was no one else inside.

"You're a wet dog," he said throwing Mark a towel. "I'll make some new coffee. This pot is old."

"I'll be drinking alcohol today," said Mark. "I don't suppose you have any quality champagne. No, I suppose not. I'll have a chalice of your finest beer then. We must celebrate. Today my big twin brother gets married. I should toast him. I should toast them."

A few hours later Mark was drunk. For the tenth time he castigated Earl for not having any Michael Bolton on the jukebox.

"It's a wedding. How can you have a wedding without Michael Bolton? Where's your sense of romance?"

Earl apologized for the tenth time and said he'd look in to getting some new songs.

"You should slow down, Mark. It's early and all."

"I should. I should, indeed. I would like to buy a round for the house."

"You're the only one here," said Earl.

"Barkeep, join me!"

Earl downed a shot of rye and Mark smiled before swiveling toward the brick wall. For the next two hours neither man spoke. Earl polished clean glassware. A few customers came, drank and left. Mark forgot about the wedding. The meat-colored wall calmed him. The etched short stories reminded him he wasn't alone. Each clay brick was a physical manifestation of possibility.

At ten minutes past ten o'clock, Earl informed Mark it was closing time.

"What do I owe you, my good man?"

"Nothing. You kept me company. It's on me."

Earl helped Mark home. It wasn't far. Mark weaved up the porch steps slowly, deliberately. Earl waited on the puddled sidewalk. He wanted to be certain Mark got safely inside. In front of the door Mark turned and thanked Earl for his kindness.

"It makes you feel alive, doesn't it?"

"What?" asked Earl.

"The rain. The incredible, glorious, warm, wet, magnificent, life-giving rain, Earl. May wondrous random raindrops forever fall on us all."

PHILIP

There was one dereliction Philip needed to rectify before the wedding. And it could not be put off any longer. He knocked loudly on the hotel room door and softly rehearsed his short speech.

"May I come in, sir?"

Kate's father gestured with an arm sweep and Philip paced to the middle of the room, turned and delivered a practiced monologue.

"Mr. Purcell, I need to apologize that I neither sought nor gained your approval to marry your daughter. I have no excuse for this omission. Please accept my sincerest apology. My timing may be unorthodox, but I ask you now for your permission and your blessing. I love Kate and want to spend the rest of my life making her happy."

Chuck Purcell grinned and sat down.

"No apologies needed, Philip. I'm not that old-fashioned. And my daughter makes up her own mind about most things. If she wants to marry you there's not much I can do to stop her. Even if I wanted to. You seem like a nice fellow. I know you come from a good family. And you and Kate make a real good-looking couple. She seems happy. So, if you need my permission you have it. But remember, it's really Kate's decision. Always will be. Treat her well, young man. She's all I have."

Philip was momentarily blinded. Sunlight bounced off Kate's satin wedding gown, starbursts exploded off her veil. Her long golden hair was electrified. It was as if the light emanated from within. She was ringed by a brilliant reflected aura. He blinked until he could make out her face. She was so beautiful. She was stunning. He felt he was the luckiest man alive. He turned and shook hands with his best man. His palms were moist. He couldn't contain his smile. The day was perfect. He looked around and wondered if he'd ever be this happy again. His friends, family, the woman he loved, the setting, it was all perfect. Even the big balloon was perfect. It was her idea. Everything was her idea. And it was, from where he stood, absolutely perfect. There was no other word to describe it. Of course he wished his father was present. He wished Mark was too. Mark is such a baby, he thought. And a coward. I saw her first, Philip remembered. I talked to her first and bought her drinks. Never once did I complain that he dated her after that. Not once. I moved on and lived my life. But can he be happy for me when the situation is reversed? No. He can't even pretend, for one measly day, to be a man about it. Let him wallow. He can rot in Iowa for all I care. I won. He lost. My happiness doesn't need him. Today is not about him. Philip spied his mother crying. Her tears were not tears of joy, he thought. She's wasting them on Mark, I'll bet. Today is not about him, he wanted to shout. Mr. Purcell marched Kate up the aisle. His grin could not have been any wider. At least he looks happy, thought Philip. I won't let anyone ruin my happiness; no one can ruin this for me, no one, not today.

After the short ceremony Mr. and Mrs. Philip Copeland walked down the petal-strewn aisle to genuine applause and boarded the awaiting hot air balloon. Much maneuvering, fabric bunching and discussion was required to protect Kate's bulky gown and long train. The guests were served champagne. The plan was that the tethered balloon would ascend above the crowd a modest twenty feet—the length of the four rope anchors—at which point everyone would raise their locally cultivated bubbly and drink to the floating newlyweds. Kate and Philip held their flutes high as the balloon climbed. The quartet played the Carpenter's "Top of the World." The valley spread out below. Half way up, the basket jerked and Kate dropped her glass, which bounced harmlessly off the trampled lawn with a thud, missing one of the flower girls by inches. When they finally reached altitude Philip lifted the flaxen liquid to the sky. The crowd followed his lead. A million bubbles danced in the afternoon sunlight. Then he lowered the flute, presented it to his bride and he and she sipped their first drink as man and wife, as one, sharing the one vessel. Philip whispered in Kate's ear that he was literally on top of the world and he had her to thank. She kissed him and they slowly returned to earth. The guests dispersed. And with a little help, and another glass of champagne, the couple and the dress alighted without further incident. Philip spent the next hour and a half painfully posing for the photographer, for Kate, and for posterity.

At the reception, after the five course meal had been eaten and praised, Philip made the rounds. He wanted to ensure everyone was having fun. He danced with his wife and laughed with his friends. He patted many people on the back, kissed many on the cheek. It was Kate's night, her party, but he was the big man in the room. It was a role he was happy to play. He was accustomed to it. As the night advanced he found himself relaxing at a distant corner table overpopulated with half empty drinks joking with Jeb and a few other Silicon Valleyans. They were talking about technology. They were talking about work. Philip lectured on his company, how it was at a critical juncture, how they couldn't let up now, how it would spell disaster, and how the best was yet to come.

"Relax, Phil, it's your wedding night for fuck's sake. Aegis'll be there in the morning," said Jeb.

"If I don't worry about these things, who will?" said Philip. "You? Aegis is my life. It's who I am."

"Not tonight it's not. Tonight you're a groom."

"Yeah, a groom who has to pay for all this. How am I supposed to do that if Aegis loses money?"

"Aegis is number one. And there's nobody close. Successful business, beautiful wife, you have it all; but it's not enough for you, is it? Slow down, take it easy, you've already won. Don't worry just to worry. It's no way to live."

Philip laughed.

"As best man," said Jeb, "I have a time-honored responsibility for your welfare this evening. Therefore, in my role as best man, you best take my best advice. Go now to your gorgeous wife. Do not tarry. Kiss her, hug her, hold her tight, and take her upstairs and do what happy newly married couples are supposed to do. Couple!"

The men laughed. Philip slapped Jeb on the shoulder and left to find Kate.

The newlyweds took the private elevator up to the bridal suite. They kissed in the corridor. Philip unlocked the door and carried Kate across the threshold. She was as light as light itself. He did have it all, he thought.

One of the two dozen digital recordings left to me by my father—recordings advising me on various topics, from respecting one's elders to finding one's purpose in life—describes his endless love for my mother. He says, and I am quoting verbatim now, 'I loved her from the moment I saw her. She was like an angel. She was the kind of being you fell in love with instantly and eternally. And I knew one day I'd get my

opportunity. I knew one day she'd be mine. In the beginning
California kept us apart; in the end it brought us together.'

JOAN

"Four years ago I was buttering his toast," said Joan.
"And now he's getting married. You know that was
the last time I saw him."

"I haven't seen Kate in just as many," said
Chuck. "California sticks to some people, I guess."

Joan sipped her white wine and looked down at
the clouds.

"I suppose I set them up. Yes, I suppose I did.
But there wasn't any ulterior motive. I just asked him
to look in on her. I put him at her door. The rest was
up to them," said Joan.

"The whole business caught me by surprise, I
must say. That's always been Kate's way. She
surprises. First it's Mark and acting, then it's not Mark
and not acting, then it's Philip and we're getting
married. I was surprised mostly. I don't know Philip
like I do Mark. Mark is a fine boy. A fine boy."

Neither had ever flown first class before. For
Chuck it was his first time on an airplane. The trip
was long but comfortable. They agreed the hot towel
they were given before landing was the best idea ever.

Joan had her own suite, another first. Philip
asked her how she liked the accommodations.

"Oh, it's lovely, just lovely. It's too big for one
person and much too extravagant, but lovely all the
same. And the view is spectacular. It's really lovely,

Philip. Thank you. There is one thing though; I can't seem to find an iron any place. Maybe you could help me look. My dress, the dress I plan to wear to the wedding, developed a few rumples on the way over. I'd like to look my best."

"The hotel will press it for you. All you have to do is ask. No, I'll call and arrange it."

"Just ask them if I might borrow an iron. That's all I need."

"Mom, show me what you want pressed and I'll take care of it."

"You have too much to do already. You must be so busy. Here, sit down, take a minute. Let's talk."

Philip sat next to his mother. She patted his knee and continued.

"Philip, you know that I am happy for you. You seem happy. And I would never want to do anything to jeopardize your happiness. But marriage is a big step. I want you to be sure. There's no need for haste. I would hate for you to make a mistake. Don't say anything. I just want you to ask yourself if Kate's the right one for you. There are a lot of women in the world. I want you to be sure. I want you to be happy, always. Remember, no matter what you do I'll always be proud of you, I'll always love you. You don't have to answer. This was more of a soliloquy, more for me than for you. I just want you to be happy. I want you to know how much I love you."

Philip thanked his mother and told her he loved her too and no one would ever replace her. Then he asked for the rumpled dress, kissed her on both cheeks and left.

Joan prayed it would be a brief ceremony. There were too many people. The sun was too intense. She hadn't brought a hat. And her chair was uneven, slowly sinking in the soft grass, which led to countless imagined scenarios of her toppling over, embarrassing herself and Philip. She envisaged streaky green and brown stains on her new freshly ironed cream dress. She hadn't packed another. She'd be forced to wear the soiled one to the reception, a dirty reminder of her mortifying fall. She tried to carefully rebalance in the wooden chair. Her left leg would soon begin to cramp, she decided. Despite all this, the main reason she hoped the wedding would soon be over was that she half worried Mark, somehow, at any moment, would appear and ruin it. Maybe Kate—and she did look beautiful, like an absolute goddess, thought Joan—would change her mind and run off with her younger son leaving poor Philip alone at the altar. No, Philip would never allow that to happen. He would fight for Kate. Her sons would battle. It was her worst fear. Joan pictured them brawling on the lawn bloodying each other, tuxedoed strangers unable to pry them apart. Philip manages to get his hands on a champagne bottle and murders his brother, his twin, unless, that is, Mark reaches it first and kills Philip. That's how easily it could happen, that's how quickly one son could be the death of the other, thought Joan, as she watched Kate glide up the aisle.

After the uneventful ceremony—Joan didn't fall, Mark didn't appear, no one was murdered—the guests were ushered into the winery's chateau and plied with the house specialty. Two sips into her

Cabernet, Joan's cheeks were bright red. People she didn't know congratulated her as if she herself had been the bride. Chuck stayed close and they asked each other, "Who was that again?" more times than they cared to count. Eventually they were seated for dinner. Joan shared the long head table with Chuck, the wedding party and the happy newlyweds. The constant tinkling of glasses, the kissing and the never-ending courses drew-out an otherwise delightful meal.

Joan waltzed once with her son and once with Chuck Purcell. That was enough, she thought. She was tired. It had been a long, long day and she was two-thirds through her fifth glass of wine. She let herself relax, listening to the band do its best with a Wilson Phillips number. The bride and groom were on the far side of the cavernous room talking to young people Joan didn't know. Chuck tapped her on the arm and introduced more business associates of Philip's. They sat and made small talk. They were young, like Kate and Philip. The man was drunk, the woman a talker. She crowed that they had been married earlier in the year. "It's a year for weddings," the young woman said. "And now, if you can believe it, I'm—we're—pregnant. It follows, doesn't it? I'm sure Kate—and Philip, of course—won't be far behind. Although—between us and the lamppost—you two look far too young to be grandparents. Ssh, don't tell my parents I said that. Caw. Caw. Caw."

Joan hadn't considered a child. She had been so concerned about her sons she'd forgotten about the grandchild. She had not placed the third prophecy among her top shelf worries. Years ago she had deemed it too awful to contemplate. It now rushed back with the woman's cackling.

She had been drinking wine with Walter. They were out to dinner in Chicago for their anniversary. The twins were with the sitter. The restaurant was a small Italian place on the near North Side. It was dark. They joked about not being able to read the menu. She had red wine and it went straight to her cheeks. Philip finished the second bottle by himself. They were having a wonderful time until he blurted out the third New Orleans prophecy. Joan was furious.

"I told you I never wanted to hear it."

"It was nothing," slurred Walter. "It was a long ago nothing. I thought you'd be over it by now. I thought you'd see the humor in it. Har."

"It isn't funny. First I have to worry about you, then the boys and now this, now a monstrous grandchild. A poor cursed baby. It isn't funny at all, Walter. Some things you don't joke about. Ever."

1996
CAUDATE LOBE
THE BEETLE

THE THIRD PROPHECY—TO *give away the punch line—is my cue. This is where I scuttle toward the stage. I am the primary—but most certainly not the only—victim of the third and final prophecy. I am the monster. I am the poor, cursed grandchild, though, as I create these chronicles, I am no longer a child and there are times, however infrequent and short-lived, I feel less than cursed. For the present this is all beside the point. We are about to raise the curtain on act 3. You must wait a bit for my emergence. Act 3 could be dubbed the highpoint of my* original *drama. (I've stressed the pun.) It is the summit of success for our leading players. They will never again attain such professional heights. In many ways they will never be happier. (It is significant I am not present to blight their brief happiness.) But there is also a great low. There is tragedy in act*

3. *Ay, there's the rub. My maternal grandfather dies amid the triumph. First Walter, then Charles—sorry, Chuck. Two deaths in three acts. Three deaths if you count my maternal grandmother's antecedent offstage suicide. (As an aside, I must admit tallying the bodies makes my story seem positively Chekhovian. At least there have been no gunshots.) But I am not here to seek sympathy. There is no need for condolences. The lonely, deformed creature penning this precursory account is no longer a child to be pitied. No, these are the memories of others. Let me remind you this is my prehistory. Outside of a few photos, some apocryphal stories and the wedding video, I never knew the man they called Charles Purcell. Regardless, he was my grandfather. I carry his DNA. He deserves my respect. He is a part of me.*

PHILIP

Kate and Philip owned identical, palm-sized, flip phones: black Motorola StarTACs. Sometimes, by accident, they picked up the wrong one. Philip had rushed out of the house late for a meeting. He'd been working eighteen hour days. His mind was elsewhere. So the first time he tried to call Kate he received an error message. He realized his mistake and redialed.

"Hey, hon, they caught the Unabomber. It was just announced on the radio. I don't know, Montana or Wyoming. Anyway, that's the big news. Wanted you to know. I'll probably be late again tonight. Don't wait up. I love you."

Philip ended the call and dropped the phone into his shirt pocket. He considered the Unabomber for a second and then weighed the thought against the eighty-eight gram instrument resting in his pocket. Why would anyone want to stop technology? Too many live in the past instead of embracing the future. Idiotic Luddites. Anyway, I should put stickers or something on them so we don't mix them up, again. Phones, not Luddites. Ha. Second time this week. I could've called the landline, instead, he thought. No, landlines and cables and wires are today's dinosaurs, fated for obsolescence. He was convinced. He was ahead of the curve.

Aegis had changed. It had been almost ten years since he had started the company. And in those ten years they'd moved offices three times, always seeking more room. Aegis had grown. It was wildly successful. Years ago he'd bought out Jeb and the other partners. And it kept getting bigger. He hired the best and the brightest to build better code, to sell his always-improving product. Aegis became a behemoth. It grew too big. It became unwieldy, sluggish. Philip found himself playing roles he'd neither sought nor wanted. His workday became about advertising and market saturation. He was counseled to worry about positioning. Philip didn't care about any of that. He had seen a technical challenge and he had conquered it. But at some point he had become a businessman. And he didn't want to be a businessman. He was an innovator. He needed to be in the vanguard. He could no longer innovate at Aegis, innovation could jeopardize the brand he was told. He had more than enough money. He could do whatever he wanted, wherever he wanted. He wanted out. It was time to sell. Thus, without informing anyone except select, trusted staff and a small legal army, he began to entertain offers for the company. It didn't take long. In less than a month he had chosen the winner. The deal would soon close. And the deal was big.

Everyone was seated when he arrived. The conference room blinds were snapped tight. Stacks of paper covered the table. They stood as he entered. They sat when he sat. Then they went over the conditions, again, line by line. Lawyer challenged lawyer. The room reeked of halitosis and furniture polish. Documents slid back and forth. Philip waited. The lawyers grinned. A final date was set. The contracts would be prepared. They all shook hands. Aegis' general counsel popped a breath mint into his wide mouth and pumped Philip's right hand with gusto congratulating him.

"You are about to be a very wealthy man," he told him.

Philip bought flowers for Kate, irises, her favorite. He brimmed with anticipation. He was home early for the first time in months. He charged into the house and boomed her name. Kate rushed in, out of breath. He handed her the flowers and burst with the news.

"Don't tell anyone. The papers haven't been signed yet. And I want everyone to be here. I want everyone to hear it at the same time."

Philip was excited, more excited than he'd been in years. But it wasn't about the money, though the amount was significant. He was galvanized by the opportunity to make a fresh start. He was intoxicated by the promise of a new future.

"We'll fly them in. Private jet. My mom. Your dad. Mark. We can tell them together. I want to see the looks on their faces. They should be here for this. Please don't say a word to anyone. I want this to be a surprise."

Joan worried about the abrupt invitation. She thought there must be a problem. She asked Philip why he was in such a rush.

"I'll explain the situation when you get here. And everything's fine. Just fine."

Mark declined the opportunity to fly on a private jet and offered to cover for Chuck at the union. Chuck wasn't comfortable leaving the keys with someone who was—however practiced and trustworthy—technically no longer employed by the college. He regretfully told Kate and Philip that he couldn't make it just now. He had commitments. He couldn't run off at the drop of a hat, no matter how fired up the hat might be.

The big family announcement then was Philip telling his mother that he was selling the company. She appeared relieved by the conventional news. He went into detail. It was the first time he'd told Kate the terms.

"It's a strange feeling, surreal. Once I sign the papers, I will retain no part of Aegis. It will belong to someone else. With the stroke of a pen—a lot of strokes, actually—I will forever waive my rights to all the patents, designs, codes, developments, basically anything I've ever created. I know. It's a lot to give up. But it's the right thing to do. And the time is now. I sign over everything and we get a new life, a new beginning. I sign and it's theirs. And in return they will pay me—in a mixture of cash and stock—a little over four hundred and fifty million dollars."

Kate dropped her coffee cup. Joan gasped. Philip grinned.

KATE

"I love you too," said Kate before depressing the tiny button and ending the call. She had no idea why he wanted to tell her about the Unabomber, the news meant nothing to her. But she liked hearing Philip's voice. She enjoyed the surprise. She hadn't seen much of him lately. There was something big happening at work. Something he wasn't telling her.

Frankly, Kate was bored in Sunnyvale. She had few friends and few outlets. She read bad books—she was currently half the way through *Angela's Ashes*—and watched bad television. She played tennis four times a week. She shopped. She thought by now she'd have had a child or two, ideally one of each. She wanted to be a mother. And she wanted Philip to be a father. She wanted a family. They had been trying for three years. She wondered whether there was something wrong with them. It shouldn't be so difficult. It's been too long, Kate decided. It was time for action. She wasn't the type to leave things up to fate. *When Philip comes home tonight I'm going to tell him we—both of us—need to see doctors. There must be something wrong, maybe it's something we can fix*, she thought.

She ended her afternoon lesson early. She'd worked on her broken backhand for ninety minutes without a breather. She hated her backhand. It was weak and errant. Whenever she could, she would scramble to her left to hit a forehand instead. Even with all the practice she didn't feel like her second best stroke was getting any better. It still felt forced, unnatural. She had had enough for the day. Kate was tired.

She was in the kitchen washing a pear when Philip yelled. Expecting disaster, she ran to him. There was an enormous smile on his face and irises in his hand. He presented the flowers and practically exploded with the news that he was selling Aegis. In his excitement she forgot to tell him about her doctor decision.

Kate tried her best to persuade her father to come out for the announcement.

"Philip would really like you here, Dad," she said. "He wants the whole family here. He wants us all together. It's sweet. Isn't there anything you can do?"

"You tell your husband I appreciate the sentiment and the private transport but I can't up and leave like that. I've made promises. I know it's not much, but people count on me. Tell him I'm sorry.

But you're okay, aren't you? There's nothing wrong, is there? I'm always here for you, don't forget that. This'll always be your home."

"I know, Daddy. I know."

Kate wasn't surprised Mark didn't join his mother. The brothers mostly ignored each other. When Kate realized Joan was the only one coming she suggested they go to them.

"The plane's going there anyway, right? Why don't we just go out to them? Wouldn't you like to see old Delphi again?"

"But this is where the news is," answered Philip. "This is where the announcement belongs. They should come to us. Anyway, there's too much going on. I can't get away, not even for a minute. It's critical. I can't compromise the deal."

The Copeland women were stunned by the figure. Philip had never hinted Aegis was worth so much. They had had no idea. When he left the room to get paper towels they promptly changed the subject. Neither one of them knew how to talk about half a billion dollars with a straight face.

"How are you, dear?" asked Joan.

"Oh, fine. It's news to me too. I guess I'll have to get used to—"

"I don't mean about the money. Or the company. I mean in general. Are you happy? Is everything all right? How are you and Philip doing? Is everything okay?"

Joan's questions reminded Kate she had forgotten to tell Philip about the doctor. She suspects.

92

She wants to know why she isn't a grandmother, thought Kate. Kate felt her womanhood was being challenged. She wants to know why we don't have children yet. She assumes it's my doing. She thinks I am to blame.

"Fine. Everything's fine. Life, you know."

"Good. That's good to hear. I worry about you. All marriages have their ups and downs. Life tends to get in the way of living, if you know what I mean. Remember, if you ever need an older woman's ear, I'm just a phone call away."

They ate dinner in San Francisco. They ordered crab legs at a giant-windowed restaurant near Fisherman's Wharf. They celebrated their good fortune. They toasted to the future. And the next day Joan flew back to Iowa.

Kate expected Philip to ease up after the announcement. Instead he worked more. He was gone before she woke in the morning and home long after she'd fallen asleep at night. She half suspected the ridiculous hours were his way of avoiding her babies-and-doctors obsession. He'd go see a fertility specialist, but it would have to wait until the deal is done, he promised. There was a lot to do before the contract could close. He worked harder than ever. Kate was lonelier than ever. She was tired of practicing her backhand and buying shoes. She decided she wanted to move after Aegis was sold. Maybe up to San Francisco, she thought. Maybe I'll take up acting again. Yes, I'll act again, unless I'm pregnant, of course.

JOAN

Joan placed the telephone receiver in its Bakelite cradle and worried about the baby, a baby existing, for the present, only in her mind. She imagined the moment of birth: a hideous, squealing, misshapen, bloody lump, emerging feet first to the silent uncomprehending horror of new parents and veteran hospital staff. According to the prophecy, her grandchild was to be born a monster. That poor innocent child. And the poor parents. Philip. Poor Kate. They have no idea what awaits, she thought. Kate must be pregnant. It's happening. Joan could envision no other news necessitating an immediate private jet. No other news would be so merrily urgent. My poor Philip. There was nothing I could've done to prevent it, she told herself. He was too far away. If it wasn't Kate it would be some other unfortunate girl. She imagined what would've happened had she tried to stop the wedding ceremony six years ago. Tragedy. She would have lost him. Not only that but she would have lost the ability to keep her sons apart. In the end she would have lost them both. She would have lost everything. No, she had made the right decision. A mother's first duty is to her children. First and foremost she must keep them safe. And maybe, she hoped, if she prevented the second prophecy from being realized the third would somehow be destroyed as well. The chain would be broken. Listen to yourself, Joan. You have been alone too long. This is absurd. That stupid tortoise may have been a stupid fluke. Prophecies are not real. They are myths. Balderdash, Walter would've said. Nevertheless she had kept her sons apart for a decade based on this balderdash. And both were alive and well. She couldn't stop now. She couldn't risk it. If it was madness then she would be mad. If it was a superstition it was one she would carry to her grave. She couldn't stop now. The stakes were too high. Poor Kate must be with child. There is no other possibility. It's been years. Unless it isn't possible, unless they're not able to conceive. For an instant Joan entertained the idea there might be something physiologically wrong with Philip or Kate, something anatomically preventing them from having children. Oh, what an awful thought for a menopausal woman. I have so many abhorrent thoughts, so many worries. This was not the plan.

Mark drove the car to the tiny airport in Oskaloosa.

"What do you think the big new is?" he asked.

"No idea," said Joan. "I don't have the faintest. They were both tight-lipped."

Mark shrugged his broad shoulders. Joan watched him drive and realized he didn't care about his brother's news. He was just being polite, making conversation. She frowned. She took no pleasure in the knowledge that she no longer had to work to keep them apart. The acrimony had ossified. She worried about Mark. Since he left his job at the student union she hadn't seen him as often. He shut himself up in his room for hours on end, writing she suspected. And he spent his nights at the Grill doing God knows what. They no longer had meals together. Joan wondered what he was doing for money. His savings must be shrinking. He had always been quieter than Philip, thought Joan. But now he seemed secretive too.

The Oskaloosa airport wasn't much more than a rusty white trailer parked next to a long slab of cracked concrete unspooled between rows of silent corn. In the near distance stood a small aluminum hangar with no door to protect three idle Cessnas. When Mark pulled up, the door to the trailer flew open and four very excited old men spilled out.

"You the Copelands? It's here. They're waiting for you."

A gleaming jet stood at the end of the runway, its small staircase resting on the tarmac. A tall man in a blue uniform waited.

"You can drive right up to it. They're waiting. We don't get many big planes here. Go ahead, drive right up. They're waiting for you. Go on."

Mark drove Joan to the aircraft and handed her small bag to the man in blue. She waved from a window as the plane zoomed down the runway. The old men waved back. She couldn't spy Mark or the car.

When Joan heard the news she was so relieved Kate wasn't pregnant it took a few seconds for her to process the number Philip had just quoted.

"Did he say four hundred and fifty million? Dollars?" she asked Kate.

"I think so."

Her premonition about the child had been wrong. She was thankful. When Philip came back into the living room she said, as if scolding him, "Philip, that's an awful lot of money."

At dinner she had a wonderful time. Philip had to help her fracture the thick crab legs. During her second glass of buttery California Chardonnay, Joan suggested that the newly wealthy and unencumbered couple would probably be starting a family soon. Philip and Kate exchanged uneasy glances. Joan ignored the tension and added, "You could always adopt. There's a young couple in Delphi—he works at the window factory—they just adopted the most beautiful little Chinese girl. Oh, she's precious."

Kate answered. "We haven't been putting off having children. We both want them. I'm sure it'll happen one of these days."

Joan drained the rest of her wine and worried anew.

MARK

Mark declined the free flight out west.

"You can tell me the thrilling news when you get back," he told his mother.

"What should I tell your brother?"

"Tell him I don't like to fly."

It's a short, curvy road from Delphi to Oskaloosa. At the halfway point the road dips down to a muddy creek, temporarily breaking the green monotony of soybean and corn fields. Mark felt the

97

speed as he accelerated into the turns. His mother asked him to slow down.

"What's the hurry, Mark? It's a private plane. It'll wait."

When he reached the strip of pavement the FAA considered an airport his mother dipped into her purse and removed a stack of twenties.

"Here, dear, take this. So you have enough while I'm gone."

"You keep it, Mom. I'm fine. You might need it in California."

"But I'll be with Philip. I won't need anything. Here, for me."

"Please, I'm fine. I don't want it. But thanks."

He drove the car down the patched runway and stopped at the short staircase. He hugged his mother and watched her navigate the metal treads. He got in the car, turned it around and headed back to Delphi. He didn't need to watch the plane taxi and take off. He could hear its twin engines roar as he drove away.

Alone in the car he sped faster. The windows were down. The wind was almost as loud as the turbojets. Mark thought about his brother and Kate. It had been a decade since he'd last seen Kate and twelve years since he and his brother had been in the same room. It wasn't nostalgia or sentimentality that made him count the years—it was surprise. He was surprised by life's pace. His memories, those old feelings, were speeding away. His mother was but a dot in the white sky flying west on a private jet to visit his brother and his wife: Philip's wife—*his* former girlfriend—that beautiful young girl he journeyed with to Los Angeles in a used Honda Civic all those years ago. She was, he thought, no longer a girl. She was no longer his. And he was no longer young. He drove faster tasting his memories, letting the past melt on his tongue like a lemon drop.

"I don't want you driving when I tell you the news," said Joan.

"You don't ever have to tell me," said Mark putting her bag in the back seat.

"Maybe I should drive," offered his mother.

At home she delivered the news about Philip and Aegis. Mark laughed out loud. It was ridiculous. It was too ridiculous for words.

"Did you say half a billion?"

"Four hundred and fifty million," corrected his mother.

"Someone is willing to give my brother half a billion dollars for a company that kills electronic bugs. Now that's priceless."

Mark couldn't stop laughing. He was happy for Philip. He was even proud of him. But the idea that anything related to computers could be so valuable was unreal. It was as if the two brothers inhabited different planets.

"Incredible. I'm glad you didn't tell me when I was behind the wheel. Just incredible."

Mark was in his room correcting a proof. His first book of short stories was scheduled for release in November. He hadn't told anyone yet. He'd kept the news about the book under wraps for more than a year and a half. He wanted to surprise them once a publication date had been officially confirmed. Maybe he didn't want to jinx the project. He flipped a page and his mind wandered to his brother's windfall. *If I didn't know better,* Mark thought, *I would say Philip was trying to steal my thunder. No, his news is news; my announcement is about second-rate stories nobody'll ever read. Besides he couldn't have possibly known about the book. Although with all his money he could have bought the information. Money can't buy you everything, big brother.* He debated telling his mother about the book. He decided if he told her now it would seem like he was competing with Philip . . . and losing, badly.

At the Grill, Mark ordered a beer and bought a shot for Earl. The bartender thanked him for the drink.

"Finally got some new music on the old jukebox, Mark. The rep came in this morning. It's all noise to me. Just got what he said was popular. Go on and play something. It's on me," said Earl, sliding a dollar over.

Mark didn't like the new music. He wouldn't relish listening to the "Macarena" over and over every night. He selected two Gin Blossoms tunes, one by Hootie and the Blowfish and another by Joan Osborne. And, although he disliked the song, he played "Wonderwall" by Oasis. He took it as a cue. He figured it was time to tell somebody.

Mark rested his elbows on the bar's wooden deck. He took a swig of beer from the long-necked bottle, set it back down, peeled off a bit of the label, tapped the foot rail twice then told Earl about his book.

"It probably won't sell more than a dozen copies."

He explained how the idea for the stories came from the Grill's brick wall.

"You should be the first to know considering it's your wall and all."

"I am honored," said Earl. "Thank you, Mark. Congratulations. Next round's on me. And don't forget me when you're famous."

PHILIP

The date was set. He would sign away Aegis on Friday. This was his last week in charge. It was an anomalous feeling for Philip. He'd always had a clear vision of the future. Come Friday, he would have nothing. Yes, he had earmarked the next eight weeks as 'New Project Selection.' And his notebook was a palimpsest of reexamined ideas, shifting milestones and concepts. But it was all too vague for comfort. He was undecided. And this was not like him.

His staff was aware something was amiss. During the morning debrief he didn't say a word. He didn't look at them. His mind wandered. He wasn't on top of them, pushing them, questioning, motivating. He spent the long day in his office organizing desk drawers and placing memories in a banker's box. Philip could feel the eyes on him. He wanted to divulge the sale and tell them it would be all right, but he wasn't sure if it would be all right, anyway he was bound by nondisclosure agreements.

Tuesday began the same as Monday. Philip pantomimed for passers-by. He opened and closed and reopened drawers and shuffled meaningless papers. The lawyers had emailed the final draft of the contract. He scanned it not really reading. He planned to sign what they told him to sign. Even though he had the agreement before him and little else to do, he wasn't going to waste his time on ten thousand words of unintelligible legalese. His mobile phone rang and saved him. It was Kate. She was crying. She was hysterical. She said she had to go to Iowa, right away. Philip tried to calm her down. He tried to understand her. She said she had to go to Delphi, immediately. She begged him to arrange a plane. She told him to come home. Her father was dead.

Iowa springtime assaulted Philip's nostrils the moment he stepped off the plane. His mother's car raced down the runway toward them. She parked, rushed straight to Kate and hugged her. Philip and the steward placed the luggage in the trunk. On the road to Delphi they got stuck behind a muddy tractor. Philip asked his mother to put up the windows and turn on the air conditioning. The manure smell was nauseating.

"Mark wanted to be the one to pick you up but I thought it would be better if it was me," said Joan. "I don't like the way he drives. Too fast."

Inside the Purcell home it smelled of death and dying, thought Philip, from crap to death. Then he reassessed the odor. No, it doesn't smell of death, just loneliness. He hadn't been in Kate's house more than twice in his life. It was small and outdated, all the rooms on one level. There was a large framed headshot of Kate balanced on an oval coffee table and an old black and white wedding photo hanging over the sofa. He told his wife to sit on the couch and he would make her a cup of coffee. He found unwashed dishes in the sink.

"Don't worry, I'll get everything. I'll take care of it. You just rest."

Kate wanted to help but Philip told her to take it easy. He told her it was just nervous energy. He reminded her that he'd made all the arrangements for his own father. It would be best if she just let him take care of everything. She needed to conserve her strength.

"It's hard enough, honey. You just rest. I could call my mom and have her come over if you want."

The funeral was held on a beautiful Thursday. The sky was wide and deep blue and the foliage brilliant seasonal green, a premature summer's day. Philip noted that the wind had changed. It was fresh and sweet—rural, not agricultural. Charles 'Chuck' Purcell had been well liked as evidenced by the gathering at the cemetery. The entire town attended. Chuck had been a Delphi man and a Wallace son. Philip and Mark were pall-bearers. Kate cried behind a black lace veil. Philip thought seeing her mother's gravestone after so many years had made it harder. He regretted never really knowing her dad. Philip was now all she had. He was her family. The Copelands, together and alone, thought about Walter. Loose dirt striking the silver casket made Philip remember the thud of his father's fat urn on the hard ground above Lake Red Rock. What a mess that had been. Different, but the same, he thought.

Kate repacked Philip's bag. The plane was returning for him that evening. He had to be in California by morning for the signing. Kate would stay to go through the family belongings and close up the house. Philip had already contacted a realtor. Kate seemed better, thought Philip. She's strong. She had changed into a pretty, light dress. He was still sometimes amazed by her beauty. He apologized again for having to leave her.

"Don't give it a second thought. I know how important this is. I'll be just fine. Anyway, you've got your appointment with Dr. Fulton on Saturday," she reminded.

Philip kissed her on the lips and told her he wouldn't forget about the appointment, no matter how much he dreaded it.

"Men are such babies. They just want some sperm. They're not asking for a limb."

"I'll send the plane back for you on Monday, around midday. I'll call."

His mother took him back to Oskaloosa that night.

"I hate leaving. It can't be helped. I'll make it up to her," he told his mother. "Take care of her, will you?" He kissed her good-bye and it occurred to him that he and Mark hadn't said more than five words to each other in almost three days. They were strangers. His cell ring knelled the notion from his head as he boarded the plane.

KATE

After the shock subsided, Kate got angry. She blamed Philip. She had asked him to deliver his 'big news' in Delphi. They should've gone to them. She would have had one last visit with her dad. She would've seen him one last time. Maybe she could've prevented it. But Philip had said no. She was angry. She blamed herself for not being a better daughter. She knew she had been selfish. She knew she'd taken him for granted. And, despite her mother, Kate had never truly considered what life would be like without family. He was the one true constant in her life. He had always been there and she foolishly believed he would be there forever. She had no idea he could leave her. And without warning. She was angry with him too.

Tucked away in the back of her father's bedroom closet, Kate found on old black veil that she assumed must have belonged to her mother. She shook it loose and tried it on. It was dated and musty but she wanted to wear it to the funeral. Philip found the smell objectionable and said it looked like it belonged to another century. He offered to buy her a new one.

By the day of the burial Kate had already said good-bye. She had accepted he was dead. It was not fair, but it was life. But at the cemetery, surrounded by all those people, she lost it. She failed to hold back the tide of tears. Her mother's grassy gravesite stood out next to her father's dark oblong pit. Now, she thought, after all this time, Mom and Dad will be back together; they are reunited, for eternity. She didn't know what it all meant. She didn't know how to process her feelings. So she cried. And crying helped.

Meg was unrecognizable. She's put on a lot of weight, thought Kate. They embraced and started to talk but were interrupted when Meg's three children, dressed in their ill-fitting Sunday finest, thought it would be a good idea to play tag among the headstones. Meg excused herself and scolded her children, grabbing one by a pointy ear.

Kate felt better after she removed the veil. She changed into a challis floral dress and her mood changed with the new outfit. She had done her duty. The public part was over. She felt relief.

To no avail Philip tried to reschedule the meeting. There was no alternative. Kate told him to go. She said she understood. And mostly she did. But a piece of her had hoped he would stay anyway, that Philip would declare in word and deed that she was more important than anything. She helped him pack. She reassured him she'd be all right. "Your family is here. And Meg said she'd stop by if she can get away."

From the window she watched Philip get in the

car with his mother. She drew the curtains and felt unloved. Now comes the hard part, she thought, packing up the memories, saying farewell, without an audience to keep me in character.

Kate was folding bed sheets when the doorbell rang. Joan and Mark stood on the porch. Mark held a massive casserole dish covered in tin foil. Joan had wine.

"We've brought dinner," said Joan.

"Mom's lasagna," said Mark. "Enough for a month."

After they'd eaten Joan wouldn't let Kate lift a finger. She refrigerated the leftovers—with attached heating instructions—and washed the dishes. Kate and Mark remembered her dad.

"He was always good to me," said Mark. "He was a wonderful man. I'll miss him."

"I know."

"Are you sure you want to stay here all by yourself?" asked Joan from the kitchen. "We've got room, you know."

"I'll be fine. It's comfortable. It's home."

"Well, at least walk with us," Joan said returning to the living room. "It's a gorgeous night. Walk with us. I'll have Mark walk you back."

"Yeah, help me walk off supper. I think my arteries have the cheese sweats," said Mark.

Mark held the door for his mother and told her to lock up. "I have my key," he said, dangling it by two fingers.

On the way back they passed the Grill.

"Fancy a drink?" asked Mark.

"I've never seen a prettier day for a funeral," said Earl. "God wanted it to be perfect."

Mark and Kate talked and drank beer. They laughed at how young the college kids looked. Kate played some music. Mark implored her not to play "Macarena." For a while they forgot about loss. They stayed until closing.

A thousand stars shimmered in the black sky. Arm in arm they walked back to the Purcell home.

"I hear you've got a book coming out," said Kate. "Earl tattled."

"Just some stories."

"You should be proud."

"Once it's published, I'll be relieved."

"You're too modest. Thank you for tonight," said Kate. "I needed it. Sometimes I miss Delphi. I miss the Grill. Oh, I know, I should get a brick in honor of my dad."

"Your memory—your father, Chuck—doesn't belong up there. It's an old, cold wall waiting to turn to rubble." Mark pointed to his head and his heart. "Keep him here and here."

Philip and unopened mail awaited Kate in California. Her husband acted thrilled to see her. He apologized again and told her the deal was done. He was all hers. He also said he'd seen the doctor as ordered. She half listened, opening sympathy cards and tossing aside junk mail. Then she unsealed an envelope from her gynecologist. She scanned the detailed report. Her examination and test results were normal. There was nothing preventing her from having a child. She refolded the results, placed them on her lap and told Philip she wanted to move.

JOAN

The day before he died, Chuck stopped by Joan's for afternoon coffee. He had left his new assistant, Mike, a junior philosophy major, in charge at the union.

"You've got to let these young people fend for themselves from time to time," he said. "They need to do things on their own. Make decisions. The only way they learn. I'll go back after this cup though. Don't want him swinging in the wind for too long."

The two proud parents talked about their newly rich children.

"That's an awful lot of money," said Chuck.

Joan agreed.

"The good Lord knows I don't know much about money," he continued. "I just hope they don't lose each other in it."

"I don't think my son knows that much about money either," said Joan. "It's all the same to him. He'll be on to the next project in no time. Money's never been the objective."

"It might be different for Kate," said Chuck shaking his head. "I hope not, but it might be."

Joan searched her memory for a sign of

impending death. It had all been very normal, she thought. He seemed fine; he seemed healthy, happy. It had been ordinary. It had been a day like any other.

The hospital had telephoned Joan. They had no number for next of kin, no number for Kate. She was the daughter's mother-in-law. Delphi was a small town. Joan recognized the voice on the other end as the tall woman with the doe eyes who gave her the card after Walter died. Joan wondered whether she still had the card. Then she called Kate.

Kate screamed when she heard the news. Joan heard the phone hit the ground. Kate was crazed. Joan pictured her pretty face twisted in grief. She felt too far away to help. She didn't know what to do, how to ease her pain. There was nothing she could say. She could only let it play out. She held the line. Eventually Kate calmed and picked up the phone.

"What happened?"

"It was his heart, dear. His heart."

Kate thanked her and hung up the phone. She and Philip were in Iowa by suppertime.

Joan was pleased they decided to stay at the Purcell's.

"You'll have your privacy," she told Philip. "It's better for Kate. It'll probably be more comfortable for everybody."

She wanted to keep the boys apart as much as possible. It would be easier this way.

Philip kept busy with the funeral arrangements. Mark helped out at home and ran a hundred small errands. Joan spent most hours by Kate's side, watching her ups and downs, listening to her try to make sense of life and death. Joan could do little to make her feel better. She made tea and wrapped her in blankets. She answered the phone and the doorbell whenever they rang. Mark and Philip, separately, would pop in every so often to check on the women. "Kate will be just fine," she told them. "She needs to let it out." They never stayed long. The only time the Copelands were all together was for meals. And they were short, silent affairs. Joan advised her sons to limit the conversation because it might upset Kate. Heads down, they picked at their plates until it was time to disband.

Though the relative proximity made her nervous, Joan was thankful the twins avoided each other on the whole without much work on her part. This time around she wasn't unduly concerned. Another sudden death was too terrible to contemplate. Not even fate could be that cruel. She believed a temporary moratorium had been declared. She figured she had karma as a shield. Her sons kept their distance. As pall-bearers they were even on opposite sides of the casket, she noted with satisfaction.

Kate appeared livelier after the funeral and after Philip left. During dinner they laughed. It was easy and natural. It was like old times, thought Joan, though without Walter there to make some abysmal, arcane historical reference. Mark and Kate looked back on their trip to California. Joan didn't catch the joke—she was in the kitchen getting more lasagna— but it had something to do with a photo on a street corner in the desert. The old man they persuaded to take their picture was incredulous that the young couple wanted themselves immortalized at such a nondescript intersection in Nowhere, Arizona.

"You're not the first weirdoes, you know. Used to be a lot more of you before they built the highway. But you're all the same. Young folks are weird, plain weird," said Mark imitating the grizzled codger.

With elder's gall, thought Joan.

"He must've said the word 'weird' a hundred times," continued Mark. "Now he was a character. Looked like he'd been prospecting silver. Straight out of central casting."

Remembering, Kate laughed loudly. Joan was nonplussed by her demeanor. A rapid recovery, she thought. This morning she was in tears. Maybe it was Philip's absence. Maybe it was Mark's presence. Joan had her suspicions.

She offered to drive Kate to Oskaloosa to catch her flight.

"Thank you, Joan, but Meg is going to take me. Thank you. Thank you for everything. Please give my best to Mark. I'm sure we'll talk soon."

Joan was disappointed. She'd wanted to question her daughter-in-law about her evening with her youngest son. She wanted to know what they'd talked about, what they'd done. Mark, per usual, was mum.

MARK

Mark stopped working at the Wallace student union the day he mailed the book contract back to the publisher. It wasn't that he thought he was suddenly too good for such labor or that he thought it time to move on. No, he had simply become busy with something else. He was under deadline to produce finished, polished work. He needed the time to write, and to write properly. And there would be revisions and edits and proofs to correct. He didn't complain. The lifestyle of an unknown writer living with his mother turned out to be ideal. His long solitary strolls got a bit longer. In the afternoons he wrote behind his closed bedroom door, safe and undisturbed. He lived. He observed. He licked walls and chattered to squirrels. He watched the hair on his arm change direction in the wind like August wheat fields, synchronized and golden. For hours at a time he'd sit in the middle of campus and let loud life splash past. He lapped up every moment he could.

He missed talking to Chuck. Sometimes he would drop in and they would eat lunch together, sitting at the counter, feigning annoyance at Mike's slow service. Chuck always ordered the number one. Mark preferred the number two. After he quit they had lunch with each other three times a week. Over time it became less often. Mark regretted the missed opportunities. He thought about the last time they spoke. It was a week before Chuck died. He had been in fine spirits, thought Mark. Spring, to Chuck, meant change. Another school year was ending, meaning a new one would soon begin. The college was in genial flux. Seniors were anxious about the real world, while the younger students already acted a year older, worrying about finals and grades and housing. Professors dreamed of the long summer break and staff patrolled deserted buildings. Chuck had laughed about the class of 1996. He was of the opinion that they were the dumbest in a decade. He told Mark about one particular coed who forgot her mailbox combination three times a year, every single year, for almost four full years. Chuck finally lost patience and had the mail held and hand delivered to her. He was looking forward to September's freshmen. He was happy.

When Mark heard the awful news of Chuck's fatal heart attack—his mom had blurted it out before he closed the door—his first emotion was disbelief. It was the same horrible feeling he had had when his father died, accompanied by the same immediate nausea. Every time someone you love dies, the first mental reaction is disbelief, the first physical reaction nausea, Mark thought. (It was also the way he felt when Kate broke his heart.)

The sudden loss of love,' he writes in his notebook, 'is as supernatural as love itself./It is the antipode of love at first sight./Its power and magic are revealed in black, not white.'

Mark had little to say to Philip. He told him he was sorry about his father-in-law. Philip thanked him and told him he was sorry too. Neither man wanted to dwell on death, neither wanted to talk. Mark changed topic.

"I hear you're a rich man."

"I've always felt that way."

The scene at the funeral was like a perfect moving picture, a Midwestern tableau vivant: blue skies, puffy white clouds, green grass, fresh black dirt, solemn acknowledgements and weathered, tear-stained faces. Kate shuffled with difficulty, stooped, her beauty hidden behind an old veil. Mark was moved. She was the widow of the world. He tried to fix it in his memory. He wanted to take it all in. His reverie was shattered by the shrieks of small children hiding among the moss-covered headstones. It was all over too soon.

The first bottle of dry Chianti made Joan's crusty, overcooked lasagna edible. The second bottle made it delicious. The conversation was better still. Kate was in good spirits and that raised everyone else's. They caught up. They reminisced. Mark talked too much, his mother's cheeks glowed a deep red. They tried not to think or talk about Chuck . . . or Walter.

Mark liked how he felt. The stars were out and what little wind there was moved through the trees without disturbing the leaves. It was a short walk back to the Purcell's. Mark wished it was longer. He liked being by Kate's side. It wasn't romance that made him want the night to last. It was comfort. It was contentment. He wanted to walk for miles. And he wanted her to walk by his side. She probably wouldn't say a word if they passed her house and just kept walking, he thought. She wouldn't object. In the end, though, he decided he wasn't being fair. He was being selfish. He canceled his plans for an evening walk. Instead he asked Kate if she wanted to step into the Grill for a drink. She agreed. Mark smiled and held the bar door for her. He had almost called it the Girll.

PHILIP

Philip set up the Copeland Foundation to protect his money and fund his next big project. He had a hundred ideas and was bombarded with thousands more. Mail arrived by the boxful and the telephones never stopped ringing. He ignored the distractions. He focused on the future. He hadn't told Kate yet but he was leaning toward the production of natural antibiotics. Although he didn't know much about the subject, it was a logical next step after developing computer anti-virus software. He had done his part to protect technological advancement; he would now turn his mind and his energies toward protecting biological advancement, protecting the human race. He imagined a fusion of computers, cells and the cosmos. But first he needed to know more. He needed more information.

In my memory box I have a magazine clipping dated December 1996. It is a brief interview with my dad. Although I can't be sure, it looks like it came from Business Week. *Regardless, the reporter wonders 'along with the rest of America' what Philip Copeland will do next. If my dad had already decided he kept it to himself.*

Reporter: 'There's talk among those in the know that your next venture will have nothing to do with computers, that it will be outside the world of technology. Any truth to that?'

Copeland: 'I am sorry but the logic of your question makes very little sense to me. We are past the historic point where one can speak of a separation between technology and everything else. The paradigm has shifted, permanently. Technology—computing, processing, information, whatever you choose to call it—will be part of whatever we humans think, do, or create, from now until we are no more. Your question is from another century. One can no longer draw a distinction between man and machine. We are one in the same in that we share the same future. It is a nonsensical decoupling. Does that answer your question?'

I don't know why anyone would have saved this interview. It's bad. It must've been my grandmother. She would've cut it out for Philip's name alone. It is not a flattering portrayal. It makes my dad seem like an ass. My dad most definitely was not an ass. Yes, he was confident. But he was not arrogant. He wasn't unkind.

Philip's sperm checked out fine. There were numbers and there was motility. There was no reason they couldn't have children. Kate wasn't convinced.

"If there's nothing wrong, then why don't I have any children?"

"I don't know. Stress? Timing? There could be a thousand reasons. It'll happen. I know it will."

"Two more years, Philip. I will give it two more

117

years. And if I am not pregnant we do something about it, in vitro, adoption, I don't care, something. Agreed?"

"Agreed."

Kate mentioned his brother's book. Philip was happy for him. They had gone their separate ways, they were no longer close, nor friendly, but Philip still wanted Mark to be happy. He was still his brother, his twin. He was glad Mark had found something that kept him busy.

"What's it called? asked Philip.
"*A Brick Window.*"
"What's it about?"
"Not really sure. I asked. 'Life' was all he said."

Philip set up generous trusts for his mother and Mark. He wanted to ensure they always had enough money. His mother didn't object, though she said she had everything she needed. But Mark was a different story. Philip knew Mark wouldn't take a dollar if he knew its origins. Or worse, he would burn it as some kind of a symbolic representation of their severed relationship. So Philip got creative. He had his attorneys contact Mark's publisher and offer them a deal. If they would, under the guise of royalties and future book advances, pass through Mark's trust, the trust, in turn, would agree to absorb any losses, present or future, arising from said distribution or Mark's publications. Even if they turned a profit on his book(s) the trust would still pay them handsomely for facilitating the unusual proposed payments. The publisher's attorneys accepted without comment.

Working from home reminded Philip of his early days in the valley. He fell into familiar habits, revived old routines. There was no division between work and living. But this time he had Kate. She didn't fit into his lifestyle. And she seemed unhappy, thought Philip. She seemed bored. They fought over the tiniest things. As a consequence Philip avoided her and worked harder.

"I can't take it anymore," she said.

"Take what?" asked Philip.

"What am I? What am I doing? You work. We don't talk. What do I do? I play tennis. I clean. I cook. I don't live."

Philip suggested a vacation.

"We can go anywhere you want."

With a wave Kate stormed out of his office. Philip threw up his hands and went back to his work.

A month later they purchased a place in North Beach so Kate could stay in the city whenever she wanted and live, whatever that meant. Philip didn't understand how being in separate places would help her get pregnant, but he didn't raise the subject. He loved her. He wanted her to be happy. She seemed better. He worried about her less. He concentrated on his research.

KATE

Kate preordered Mark's book. She wanted to read it as soon as it became available. She wanted to see if she'd recognize herself in any of the characters. She wondered if he thought of her. One day she would have him sign it. The book was to be delivered to the North Beach residence. Since they'd bought the condominium—the realtor snobbishly called it a penthouse—she'd spent most of her time there while Philip stayed in the valley, his face presumably lit by the weak blue glow of multiple computer monitors.

Kate got accepted into a community theater troupe on Sutter Street, the San Fran Players. Her two forgettable television commercials had not hurt her application. In the beginning she was assigned bit roles, walk-ons without lines: girl at table, woman on bench. She also answered the telephones and sold subscriptions. It wasn't glamorous, she told herself, but it was better than working on her backhand or cleaning an immaculate house.

She even made a friend, her first real female friendship since Meg. The friend's name was Rose and she was a psychic/actress. Most everyone at the theater had a *real* job, Kate being the exception. Rose looked a bit older than Kate but had the kind of face that made it difficult to ascertain her age accurately. They had been up for the same role—a part neither had won—and, as if to forget, they had shared a commiseration drink and a laugh over the casting director's third-rate choice. Their schedules were similar. They took turns answering the theater phones. Together they hawked tickets on the street corner and helped the principals with their greasepaint. They drank cups and cups of coffee and they talked. Kate told her about Mark's book and that her husband was in computers and spent most of his time out of town. Rose said she came from theater stock. Her parents had both been actors. Kate stopped wearing her wedding ring. It was common practice among actresses. She told herself she didn't want to lose it.

I have a 1998 playbill for the San Fran Players production of Harold Pinter's Tea Party. *The brochure is only eight pages long and most of that is advertising. But tucked amid offers for reduced price massages and free sides with the purchase of an entrée are the company's bios. The director wears a fedora, a scarf and a sneer. Under his artistic visage are coast-to-coast lifetime credits. There's a tiny black and white snapshot of Rose/Diana next to an oil change coupon. She looks pensive and kind. Under her picture it states that Rose is a San Francisco native and has been acting since the age of twelve when she was cast as Little Orphan Annie. Her San Fran Players appearances include Peaseblossom in Shakespeare's* A Midsummer Night's Dream *and member of The Chorus in Sophocles'* Antigone. *My mother's photo—unfortunately situated next to one of the massage ads—displays a seductive smile. Kate was Wendy. Under her grainy image it says, 'Kate has a theater degree from Wallace College in Iowa where she starred as Nora Helmer in Ibsen's* A Doll's House *and played the eponymous lead in Strindberg's* Miss Julie. *She was the court stenographer in our recent production of Aaron Sorkin's* A Few Good Men.*'*

Rose was a good listener and it wasn't long before Kate found herself in a Mission District second floor apartment having her future divined. Kate didn't believe in psychics but her friend insisted and seemed sincere. What's the harm? she thought. Rose flipped over jumbo cards. She told Kate she had an ancient, sad soul. The cards told her she was upset with her husband. There was bad blood in their marriage. Kate laughed and protested that she loved her husband but admitted to Rose that, perhaps, just perhaps, she harbored some residual anger because he had left her so quickly after her father had been buried. Rose nodded and said her father had been a successful man, not in monetary terms but spiritually. He was taken too soon. His had been a happy life, but one not without adversity. Kate didn't tell Rose about her mother. She didn't speak of her mother.

Rose had never once asked Kate for money. The readings, the analyses, her psychic insights, were all gratis. "A gift of friendship," she said.

One evening, after rehearsal, they drank tea at Rose's round, red-clothed table. Rose did most of her business at night but this particular night happened to be slow. She had no regulars scheduled. She explained to Kate before they started that should the bell ring she would have to quickly exit via the back stairs. She didn't want potential customers to see she'd been socializing.

"They like to imagine I spend all my time consulting the cards or star charts or communing with the departed."

Rose asked Kate about her dreams. Kate struggled to remember.

"There were bugs, I think."

"What type of insects?" asked Rose. "It is

important we be specific."

"Beetles, black. And there was also a lady bug."

Rose had all the information she required.

"A beetle, you may not be surprised to learn, is often associated with material well-being. And in this world, we see material attainment as a positive trait in society; therefore your dream signifies that it is important to trust the universe in all that it provides."

Kate tried not to smirk.

"And dreaming of a lady bug indicates part of your personality is invisible to others and probably needs to be uncovered in order for you to move on in the future. The black beetle shows you have many options in a project going forward. A black beetle is also the sign of magic and trouble."

When Kate got home Mark's book was waiting in the mailbox.

JOAN

Mark handed the blue, rust and gold bound book to his mother.

"What's this?"

Mark was silent. He lowered his eyes. Then she noticed his name on the spine and released a syllable of delight.

"Oh, Mark, this is wonderful. You wrote this? Oh, I'm so proud of you," she said opening it up. Mark had penned an inscription. She read it out loud.

'Dearest Mother, Whatever life my words may have, whatever fate befalls my characters, whatever future awaits my tales, let it be said they were revealed by the light of your love. I'll never be able to thank you enough. I love you. Your son, Mark.'

Joan was touched. She would have cried had Mark added another word. She didn't know what to say. She hugged him instead. Mark returned the embrace. For a second or two Joan remembered Walter's little liver book and the promise it had held all those years ago. She hoped Mark's effort would have more success. She knew it would. Walter would have been overjoyed knowing his son was a published author. Father and son would have had so much to say to each other, so much to share.

"I'll cherish this forever. I cannot wait to read it. What's it about? Don't tell me. You're not going to leave me now that you're a published writer, are you?"

"Don't worry, Mom, I'm not going anywhere."

Watching him pad up the stairs Joan questioned how she'd spent the past twelve years of her life. Or, more specifically, she questioned what she had done to the lives of her two remarkable sons, how she had played on their sympathies, how she had manipulated events and emotions. And, why? For what? Because she believed that the words of a few puerile New Orleans coeds were prophetic? Because she accepted the idea that fate was real? Because of a turtle logo on a truck? No. She had driven a wedge between her twins because she was a mother who loved her children above all else. She had done it out of love. She had had no choice. Any good mother would have done the same. Why take the chance? She kept her sons separated because she wanted them to be safe.

She kept them separated for their own welfare. She kept them separated because she was afraid of what would happen if she did not.

Writing this I realize—I do—that I have painted my grandmother as a woman in constant dread. Perhaps this is unfair, but it is not unintentional. Her fear is what I remember most. She was never without it. Once, when I was nine, she plucked me from the bottom step of a workman's ladder and admonished me for such death-defying behavior. After she had calmed herself down and realized I was safe, she apologized, confessing, 'Your grandmother wouldn't know how to live without her worry.' Certain childhood moments are never forgotten. And destiny is not born without memory.

Philip phoned and explained the trusts he was initiating. He was calling from his car and the crackling of interference irked Joan. She wished he'd use a regular phone like everyone else. He told her the process was already begun; there was nothing she had to do. The money would automatically appear in her account.

"But I don't need your money," she said.

"Mom, it would be more work to undo it," pleaded Philip. "Don't spend it if you don't want it. Please, for me."

He told her about his concerns regarding Mark's trust and his complicated plan to keep him in the dark. Joan told him she didn't want to know the details.

"He won't need your money either," she said. "I'm sure his writing career will prove lucrative."

"I'm sure it will," said Philip without sarcasm.

125

The call ended midsentence before his mother had the opportunity to ask him about his plans for the future. Joan cursed cellular telephones. She wanted to know if he'd decided. She was concerned he hadn't selected his next great project. Philip needed a purpose. She started to worry that he may never find anything like the anti-virus computer idea, but soon shifted her concern to Kate. She was still childless. She must be out of her mind, thought Joan. Bored and out of her mind. Maybe she'll never have a child. Maybe my grandson will be Mark's offspring, not Philip's. Maybe there will be no grandchild. Maybe. I can't protect everyone from everything.

Mark was out for the evening. At the Grill, probably, Joan thought, or out for one of his long walks to nowhere. She uncorked a bottle of wine and poured herself half a glass. She got comfortable on the sofa and flipped open her inscribed volume of *A Brick Window* and began to reread. This would be her third time through her son's beautifully sad stories. They kept getting better. There was always something she had missed. Alone, she sipped Barbaresco, her cheeks rose red.

MARK

The book about bricks felt weightless in his hands, as if it would float off into the clouds should he relax his grip. He turned the tome, slowly, letting the light play with the cover's colors. He was afraid to open it. He knew the flaws contained within. He knew every word by heart. And now they were preserved for posterity. He was unnerved by its existence. It made him queasy.

He wrote a brief note to his mother in one of the advance copies and presented it to her. He was happy she didn't gush and make him feel more awkward than he already felt. They hugged and he ran up to his room. He hoped they'd never speak of the book again.

Mark had promised Earl a copy. He scribbled a dedication and set out to deliver on his promise. The autumn afternoon was brisk and bright. It seemed a shame to spend it in a fetid, dark barroom. So Mark and the book went for a walk. His legs were strong and he felt younger than he had in years. The breeze was at his back and he reckoned he could hike all the way to Lake Red Rock. Instead he crossed the square, passed the cinema and the liquor store, and headed for the open road. Two hours later he turned around to look back from where he'd come. In the undulating distance he could make out the giant Walmart pinned to the northern edge of town. If he kept walking he'd get to Des Moines in a day or two. He sat down by the side of the road between the minced farm fields and the scavenging crows. The sun was well on its way west to California. Every few minutes a car would speed by, the driver no doubt wondering what the foolish young man with an unopened book was doing on a county route's shoulder in the middle of the Iowan nowhere. Mark waited, watched and listened. He held the book up to the sky blotting out the sun. Then he stood, brushed the gravel from his bottom, and returned to Delphi.

The plan had been to give the book to Earl without a fuss, without anyone else around. But by the time Mark reached the Grill it was early evening and crowded. He considered postponing the task. The book got heavier in his hands. He went in to unburden himself.

Mark found a seat at the bar on a shaky stool near the bathroom. Earl was busy filling pitchers—both taps were open—and hadn't noticed him. A sticky tray of snakebite shots sat unclaimed next to the register. Mark set the book on the bar hiding it between his forearms. Earl saw him and made the sign for coffee. Mark nodded.

"Here you go."

"And here you go," said Mark sliding the book to Earl.

"Well, well," said Earl without opening it, "here it is. Thank you, Mark. I'll put it up where it won't get wet. We'll talk about it later. Okay? The youths are thirsty tonight. Let me know when you want a refill."

Mark sipped his coffee, listened and observed. The Wallaceans were getting drunk, a few were leaning against the brick wall reading the scratches and roaring. He remembered what it had been like as a student. He remembered what it had been like to be young and free and happy with possibility behind every smile, laughter after every joke. It was a never to be repeated four year burst of exuberance. Mark still had the desire. But he no longer had the energy or the constitution. He watched, cringing in sympathy as they drained shots and danced the "Macarena."

The song had played twice since he'd arrived and they were running poor old Earl ragged. They spilled drinks on one another and happily licked the wetness away. Mark was set to signal for a refill when a pretty young woman, too mature to be a student, asked if the seat next to him was taken.

"No, it's all yours."

Mark gestured to Earl who hadn't noticed the woman.

"What'll you have?" he asked, wiping his hands on the gray towel hitched to his belt.

"Beer please."

"Mark? Another cup."

"I'll have a beer too. And let me pay for this young lady's."

The woman thanked Mark and they talked over the cold beer. Her name was Emma and she was a new history teacher at Wallace. An adjunct, she felt the need to add, not a real professor. Mark mentioned his father had also taught history. She asked his name. When Mark said 'Walter Copeland' she exclaimed, "Certainly not the Walter Copeland who wrote the liver book?"

"I'm afraid so."

When Emma said it was time for her to leave, Mark asked if she would like an escort. Under a gibbous moon they strolled down the quiet Midwestern streets. She didn't live far. Nothing was far from anything in Delphi. At her door she leaned in, stumbled slightly and kissed him good night. Her mouth was soft and warm.

On his way home, the taste of excitement and sweetness still on his lips, Mark wondered whether he had another book in him. Every man is the child of his own deeds, he reminded himself. Cervantes. What was his next deed, he mused. He was not too concerned. I'll do what I always do, I suppose. I'll live.

There's a fine line from A Brick Window *that has always stayed with me. And it is apropos. The sentence is from a story entitled "Appointment for Tomorrow." Mark writes, 'A first kiss is absolute; it is an eternal promise fulfilled.' Isn't that lovely? Of course I have never known a romantic first kiss and most likely never will, but that is how I imagine a first kiss to be, absolute and eternal.*

2002
QUADRATE LOBE
THE SNAKE

I WOULD HAZARD A guess that most monsters—presuming they have the requisite motor skills and intellect—are great readers. I know I am. Scorned by society we live alone with our thoughts, forced to construct tolerable realities. We are left with little else. And the stories help. They ease the pain and the loneliness. After all, monsters do not have friends; we do not play well with others.

When I was younger, I was obsessed with the novels of a now very famous author. (I prefer not to disclose her name. There was an incident. Litigation. A small settlement. The specifics no longer matter.) Anyway, I adored her books. I reread them until the pages fell out. I made puppets to resemble her characters. I built dioramas of her scenes. I could not get enough of her imaginary worlds. In bittersweet anticipation I

131

lived for every new release. I marked my calendar. I—or, rather, my mother—procured advance copies that came in sturdy brown paper which I shredded with eager abandon. I inhaled her words. I loved, fought and died with her heroes, clowns and villains. I could not get enough. For my birthday—I forget which one, thirteenth or fourteenth, I suspect—my mother presented me with a leather-bound signed copy of my idol's latest novel. Thick with a forest green cover, treble ribbed spine and gold-tipped pages it arrived shrink-wrapped with an attached certificate of authenticity. It was without question the greatest present I'd ever received. I loved it with a fervid religiosity. I considered it sacred, beyond special. I slept with it underneath my bed. I dusted it every day, careful not to injure the protective plastic. I transported it on my fingertips like a waiter holding a serving tray. I cherished it. I took care of that book as if it was a pet, a living, loving creature. For beneath the thin film of plastic, inside the soft green cover, lived a wonderful, secret world of words signed by its godlike creator. It was too precious. And do you want to know something? To this day I've never opened that present. (I bought a second copy—unsigned, not gilded—and read and reread the replica instead.) I've always treated the signed edition with reverence, never sullying its perfection. I could never muster the mettle to pierce its shielding skin, exposing what is mortal and unsure. The book would die. It would degrade, devalue. The signature would start to fade. And I would be the one responsible. I still have the gift, the book. And it remains safely preserved in its original plastic. I dust it every other day. The author's signature and the gold-tipped pages are as secure and pristine as they were the day I first held it in my trembling adolescent hands. At least that's what I assume. That is what I believe. Sometimes, though, I wonder whether or not the book is actually signed at *all. How would I know? What if there is nothing inside? What if the pages are blank, devoid of rhythm or scene or character? What if I've been duped? And, even more disturbingly, what good is a never opened gift? If I've never seen what's inside, what do I really possess? Act 4 of my prehistory generates similar questions. I'll do my best to stay out of the action. It works better that way I think. I am a better director than actor.*

Enter stage right a sick man, my father. He is now almost forty years old.

PHILIP

I'm too young to feel this old, thought Philip; I have too much to do. It was nine in the morning. He lurched to the desk, clicked a wireless mouse and squinted.

The American doctors gave him the same story the German doctors had. 'Your liver has been irreparably compromised. It is damaged beyond its abilities of self-repair. With care and rest and healthy living the organ may continue to function for another five years, maybe seven, at which point you will require a transplant.' There was no debate, no alternate prognosis. There was no other possibility. And this is all I get from the most renowned hepatologist in the free world, he thought.

"When that moment comes I'll get a new liver," he told them. "In the meantime, I have a life to live." But he hadn't factored in the constant lethargy, the relentless lack of energy. He had the will, not the power. He told his wife it felt like he was running on batteries that never quite charged. He was fatigued, day and night, no matter how much he rested, no matter how slowly or little he moved.

Kate did what she could to make life easier for him. She brought him food and drink and made sure his laptops were fully charged. She saw that he napped in the afternoon and went to bed early at night. She tried to make him happy every way she knew how. They had more sex than they'd had in years. Kate did all the work. She blames herself, Philip thought. It's no one's fault.

They had been living in Berlin when he collapsed. The story of his illness, though, began earlier. It began in Fiji.

He and Kate had jetted off to paradise to escape their stressors. Philip couldn't decide on his next big mission. And Kate couldn't stay pregnant. It had been hard. They both needed a break. They needed to relax.

Their bungalow on the water rented for five thousand dollars per day. Blues and greens of water and sky mixed and melded as the Copelands held hands listening to birdcalls and palm frond music. Kate read. Philip thought. They had no neighbors, no distractions. They rested.

A week into their stay they were invited by resort management to attend an exclusive traditional island sharing ceremony. They accepted out of politeness. Philip and Kate were the only westerners in attendance. They were given seats of honor at the head of a long, stained, wooden table. They felt like interlopers. Attentively, apprehensively, they studied the tropical ritual and watched as the communal cup slowly approached. A clap, swallow the contents and three more claps. The strange brew placed before Philip looked and tasted like muddy water: bitter, muddy water. He passed the cup to Kate with a shrug. Ten minutes later his anxieties melted away into the warm breeze. Everyone spoke at once. The dancing and music and laughter lasted long into the starry night. He later asked about the drink. "We call it yaqona. The world knows it by the name kava. Kava is a Tongan word. Yaqona has been part of our culture since the sky met the sea," said a grinning, cross-legged, wrinkled old man. Philip was impressed. He had never been a drinker, never done drugs. The bitter-tasting concoction put him at ease without dulling his senses. In fact he thought his mind had never been sharper. He experienced a calm, clear understanding. Kate's wide grin suggested the same serene euphoria.

Every afternoon, for the remainder of their Fijian holiday, Philip and Kate enjoyed the effects of the local yaqona, the kava. They lolled like natives. It was the happiest they'd seen each other in years. It was the vacation they'd both needed.

Returning to the real world revived their problems. They'd committed to spending a year in Germany so Philip could study firsthand the latest European antibiotic technology. He still couldn't decide what to do next. He wasn't sure if developing natural antibiotics was his future. He wasn't sure about anything. The peaceful island glow quickly faded in the gray Berlin winter.

Worried about her husband, Kate ordered some kava extract online. She'd researched the topic and was confident she could replicate island warmth in icy Germany. The website claimed the kava was cultivated and processed in Tonga, ancestral home of the magical root. Three weeks after she began serving the beverage, Philip was rushed to the hospital. His liver was failing.

MARK

If anyone can live without a liver it's my brother, thought Mark, gall and all. He'd heard about the supposed illness from his mother but the news didn't seem very important at the time. Mark presumed she was exaggerating for his benefit. She had always been dramatic. On the other hand he didn't doubt his brother was sick and suffering. It was a consequence of his lifestyle. His malady has its roots in rootlessness, Mark decided. My brother is impaired because he is a man without a cause. He scours the planet on a chimerical crusade. His search is pointless. Mark pictured Philip as Prometheus tied to a boulder, an eagle shredding his liver only to watch the liver regenerate and the eagle return, day after agonizing day. My brother is becoming, almost literally, the Greek god of fire, he thought. Too close to the sun like Icarus.

But it wasn't envy or contempt that made Mark

doubt the seriousness of his brother's disease. Rather it was isolation, the years and years of separation, the years he had been alone in Iowa. Mark was immured with his thoughts. He was losing his humanity. He was antisocial. He was misanthropic. He spoke to his mother. He spoke to Earl. And that was all.

Mark's sudden and unlikely celebrity had made him even more reclusive. His book had been a small critical success and continued to sell. Still, it was a literary short story collection with modest expectations. His style had not been praised. His characters were soon forgotten. His narratives had not made him famous. What had made him famous were his predictions. Mark's distinction, it seemed, was prescience.

An article appeared in *People* magazine in February 1998—Mark had declined the interview with the reporter, a determined young woman trying to make her mark on his name, he assumed—detailing six fictional events from *A Brick Window* that had later transpired almost exactly as written. This initial article dubbed him a modern day Nostradamus. Mark considered the idea absurd but couldn't deny the coincidences. His very first story, for instance, imagined the fall of the Berlin Wall years before it fell. And "Devil in the Blue Dress" depicted a United States president having an affair with a chubby, dark-haired intern named Monica. Similar articles followed, every year or so another would appear in the national press. But the coup de theatre was when two terrorist-piloted commercial airplanes destroyed New York's Twin Towers just as predicted in "Down to

Heaven." Overnight he was notorious. Fanatical readers and conspiracy theorists identified eight (in twelve tales) significant and unexplainable instances in which what Mark wrote came to pass. Some hinted at more. Others studied *A Brick Window* and tried to divine the already written future. Many believed he had seen the days to come.

People wanted to know about him. There was minor hysteria. More than one respected source unoriginally proclaimed him the Oracle of Delphi. They wanted to interview him; they wanted to know his secret. They wanted to be near him. Some wanted just to touch him. Back and forth and back again they passed in front of the Copeland house, night and day. They sat on the lawn and waited. They scaled the backyard fence. People stopped in Delphi on their way to other places. Wallace College saw a spike in applications. Earl had Plexiglas installed over the brick wall to protect the book's inspiration. Mark was under siege. He was trapped. He stopped answering the door and the telephone. He stopped taking long walks. And he ventured out to the Grill infrequently, always late at night. On occasion Earl had to act as a bodyguard, hustling Mark out the back door. He hid like a thief.

It had been five years since he'd had any kind of relationship. He no longer trusted anyone. He and Emma had dated for almost a year before her contract expired and she moved on to another school. They both thought it best—logical—to end it there. It had been a fling, thought Mark. She reached out to him after he'd become infamous but he ignored her messages. He wrote new stories in his room and took care of his mother. They even began playing Scrabble together. One day his publisher sent him an enormous advance on his next book. Mark wasn't sure there would be a next book.

JOAN

Joan felt trapped too. She was tempted to join Philip and Kate in California. She had heard the worry in Kate's voice and the frailty in Philip's. But she couldn't or wouldn't leave Mark alone. Not with all the trespassers and lunatics lurking about. Not now. Not with her youngest son afraid to leave the house. She was torn.

Worse yet she found herself half believing in Mark's powers of prophecy. She had read the articles written about him. She was familiar with his stories. As a result she began to wonder if indeed her family possessed some awful clairvoyance. The Fates had been right about Walter who had written a book on divination and now Mark had the sight. It couldn't be chance. There was more at play than meets the eye, she thought.

One evening after dinner she tried to test her theory. In the middle of their second game of Scrabble—Mark had won the previous dual, as he always did—she brought up Philip.

"Mark, what do you think about your brother? Should I be worried? Do you think he's sick sick?"

Mark spoke without looking up from his tiles.

"I don't know. He's got money. The doctors will want to keep him alive. I wouldn't worry too much."

Joan blamed herself for her son's indifference. She had turned the twins into adversaries.

"But what do you think will happen to him?"

Mark's eyebrows formed a circumflex.

"How would I know?"

"You seem to know so much," she said, wondering whether she'd gone too far.

"What does that mean?"

"It just means I would like your opinion."

"I don't have one."

"Well, what's your guess? What do you predict will happen?" she prodded.

He hesitated.

"Yes, Philip's going to die. We all are."

Joan was silent.

Mark added: "Are you asking me for the time and the date? Or is it the cause you're after? Okay, if not today then it'll be tomorrow and so on and so on. And if it's not his liver it'll be something else."

He stopped and looked her in the eye. Tears welled.

"It's your turn."

Later that night Mark knocked on Joan's door and apologized.

"I'm sorry, Mom. I shouldn't have snapped at you. But I have no idea what the future holds. I'm sorry."

The next morning Joan telephoned Philip and told him she would not be able to come out to

California. She was needed in Delphi.

"Who asked you to come?"

"Kate. She said you were ill. She said it was your liver."

"I'm fine. A little tired. Yes, there was an incident in Germany, but I am fine now. It was nothing. Kate shouldn't have said anything."

"She loves you and so do I."

"I know."

"Philip, it's okay to ask for help."

"I know that too. I'll ask for it if I need it. But I'm fine."

Philip passed the phone to Kate who spoke breezily to Joan until her husband had safely left the room.

"He's not fine, Joan," said Kate.

"I know. I can hear it in his voice. But he doesn't want me there."

"He doesn't know what he wants. He's scared. And he's afraid to admit he's scared. I'm doing everything I can to help him. I don't know what else to do."

Joan returned the receiver to its cradle. Mark entered the kitchen and poured himself a cup of coffee.

"Who was that?"

"Kate. And Philip."

"It's a little early for them," said Mark. "Are you that worried?"

"Always."

"Philip will be fine, Mom. If it was anything serious we'd know."

Joan watched her son sip his coffee. She knew the illness was serious. She didn't want to say it out loud. And she couldn't help wondering how Mark fit into Philip's malady. Maybe he didn't. Maybe the Fates had been wrong. After all the third prophecy depended on a grandchild and that possibility was becoming more remote with every passing day.

"I suppose you're right," lied Joan. "I suppose we would know."

KATE

Kate learned later—too late, one always learns the truth too late—that the commercialized kava she'd ordered was hastily processed and of poor quality. The extract had been contaminated by the plant's leaves, stems and bark. She learned—again too late—that only the root should ever be ingested. The other parts of *Piper methysticum*—she later read—contain unsafe levels of liver destroying toxin. Philip's liver had not been able to metabolize these toxins. Kate had, in effect, poisoned her husband.

All she'd wanted was to make Philip happy. He had been so peaceful and kind and content and attentive in Fiji. They'd fallen in love all over again. It was like that first week in her apartment in Reseda. They smiled again. They were happy and relaxed and together. They held hands and made love twice a day. She was confident they were creating a family.

But Berlin shattered the dream. She wasn't pregnant. She worried anew that she'd never have a child. And bit by bit Philip lost his spirit. He fell into old deceptions and threw himself in twenty different directions. Life became work. He forgot about Kate.

Before she left California people told her she'd love Berlin. They explained how German and English were related. They promised her the Berliners were hip and edgy, artsy. She found them either pretentious or boring. Their harsh accents visited her in nightmares, yelling at her, ordering her to do something in a language she couldn't begin to understand. The recently reunified city was large, monumental, but cold and soulless. No one seemed to be enjoying themselves. No one was having fun. Her life in Germany was like Sunnyvale without the good weather and bad backhand. Ironically her last month in the city—spent almost entirely in a private hospital nursing Philip—had been the best. They were again together, night and day; she looked after him, no one interfered. Doctors came and went. It was the happiest she'd be in Berlin. She had books to read and she had Philip. They planned on returning home soon, when he was strong enough. The anticipation of a homecoming was probably behind much of her relative happiness.

At first, as Philip lay weak and suety in the mechanical bed, Kate tried to persuade him that they should move to Delphi when they got back to the States. "You can work from anywhere," she'd reminded him. "And the house is sitting empty. Your family is there. We'll have plenty of help." But the nearest decent hospital was forty miles away in downtown Des Moines. It couldn't be Delphi. Philip wanted to go back to Sunnyvale. He said he felt most comfortable there. He could work well there. Kate dreaded the idea. And it was too far from the specialists. They compromised and agreed on North Beach. It was near the hospital and the doctors. And everything they needed could be found in San Francisco.

Kate went to see Rose on her third day back. She was Kate's only real outlet. They talked about acting and the San Fran Players. Rose was still with the company but she was thinking of leaving. The medium business had been booming since just before the millennium and she found it difficult to get away to the theater. It was hard to find the time to rehearse. She was making good money. Kate said she was happy for her.

"You don't appear happy," said Rose. "You said he was better."

"He's better. But he's not good. He's so feeble, Rose. It's like he's a different person."

"Some recoveries take longer than others."

"I don't know if he'll ever recover."

"It must be hard on you."

"I do what I can. I do what he lets me do, I should say."

"You don't deserve it."

"Oh, I don't mind taking care of him," said Kate. "I don't mind that at all. Do you want to know what's worse?"

"Only if you want to tell me."

"All I can think about is my child, my children. I don't mean the ones I lost. I mean the ones I want.

I look at Philip and I can see he's dying on me. Death is winning. There's nothing I can do to stop it. I need to have his child. I need my child. It's all I can think about. So, every night in bed, before he's had time to fall asleep, I get him hard with my hands and then carefully and gently mount him and ride until he comes inside me with a pitiful, infirm gasp. And the entire time I'm sliding up and down on his cock, thrusting my hips, arching my back, groaning and squeezing, I tell myself I'm making Philip happy, that the sex, the pleasure, the release, is making his life a little bit better. But that's not why I'm doing it. The real reason I fuck him every night is to get pregnant before he dies. Isn't that awful? It's awful. I'm awful."

"No, you're not."

"I am. And, even though I know I am, I can't stop. I won't."

At the beginning of this act I pledged to do my best to stay in the wings. I cannot, however, allow the crude language of the preceding section to pass without comment. For what sort of son puts the word 'cock' and 'fuck' in the mouth of his mother? I do. I do so for the sake of fidelity. I promised at the outset to be truthful. And my mother, Kate Marie Copeland, one fuddled evening when I was seventeen, used these exact words as she slurred her story about guilt-ridden sex with my ailing father. This is her tale. Not mine. Yes, you might counter, but what kind of son repeats it, exposing his mother to the entire world? I do. Remember, I am a monster.

145

PHILIP

His malfunctioning liver wasn't Kate's fault. He never once condemned his wife. Germany would have been a bust even without the collapse. He had been the one who'd decided where and when they would go. His indecisiveness was at the center of the problem. His affliction was a confluence of errors.

Whether because of the illness, Kate, Germany or Fiji, when Philip got back to California he concluded that developing natural antibiotics was not his next big project. He didn't have the necessary passion. He couldn't commit. It had taken him six years to reach a decision. He'd wasted a great deal of time. He needed to think bigger. He needed a greater goal. He needed an ultimate purpose, a final cause.

One of the areas he'd dabbled in and supported since selling Aegis was a fledging anti-death group called Athanatos. The group, created in 1999, was an inter-disciplinary team of eminent neurologists, biologists, doctors, futurists and various subject matter experts organized for the sole purpose of retarding and, one day, *preventing* human death. Their mission, simply put, was to save humanity from the ultimate disease, death itself. He had donated a few thousand dollars and met once or twice with their director, the bearded and excitable Dr. Stuart Clairday. In Philip's mind the group had always seemed too fringe, too radical and impractical, a debate society more than anything else. He now changed his mind. He had found his cause. There is nothing greater than preventing death, he said to Kate nodding his head. Everything else is secondary. Athanatos had produced a series of white papers in which they made grand pronouncements and rosy predictions. But they had done nothing concrete. They did not possess the resources. Philip would change that.

The days were short. He rose late and retired early. He ate well and frequently. He heeded doctors' orders. He took naps. As the days passed he accustomed himself to the lassitude. He adapted. He could afford to. Kate did the errands. He barely had to budge. He typed on the computer keyboard and spoke on the cellular telephone. He never left the penthouse. No one visited.

He worried about Kate. He insisted she go out into the world, visit friends and live life. He didn't want her to martyr herself in his name. She'd already done so much. He sometimes fabricated deliveries just to get her out of the house. Alone, he imagined he was slowly wrecking her life, stealing her youth. He even dreaded their nightly sex sessions. They felt like performances. They felt like work. He felt like a john.

In order to further conserve his energy Philip created the concept of micro-meetings. These were short telephone conversations—a hard stop after fifteen minutes—on one very specific topic. No tangents, no chit-chat, nothing extraneous or off-topic. Apart from Kate and his mother, he dealt with everyone via micro-meetings: accountants, bankers, CEOs, attorneys, charities, hedge fund managers; they all learned to communicate through micro-meetings.

Philip informed Dr. Clairday that he was to become Athanatos' principle backer and savior. They would have as much money as they needed.

"Mr. Copeland, I don't know what to say. I don't know how to thank you."

"Call me Philip, please, and you can thank me by using the money wisely and effectively."

"Certainly."

"My sole stipulation is that three times per week you and I speak on a topic of my choosing—of course it will be related to your work and you will be sent the day's issue in advance—during what I call micro-meetings, a concise fifteen minute conversation designed to answer my questions on the selected subject. If that is acceptable I will open my wallet. If not, let me know now so that I may pursue alternatives. These are my terms."

"Your terms are acceptable and generous."

"Excellent. I will be in touch. And, Dr. Clairday, I am placing my trust in you. I hope I will not be disappointed."

"With sufficient resources I am certain we will make tremendous progress. Mortality will one day be found only in dictionaries and history books. That is the future. I can see it."

"I understand," added Philip.

"You see it's the promise of telomeres," Dr. Clairday enthusiastically began. "Lengthening our telomeres would—"

"I'm sorry. Time's up. I will be in touch."

Philip ended the call and, for the first time in his life, admitted he was chasing someone else's vision of the future. For almost forty years he had relied on his own. Maybe each of us gets only one vision, he thought, one glimpse of the future. And for anything more we have to depend on others.

MARK

Mark woke bit by bit. He blinked several times and stretched his arms and legs noting the sensation. He started to sit but thought better of it, collapsing back into down pillows. At this stage most people would begin to brood about the day ahead. Not Mark. He yawned once then popped out of bed and into the shower. His mind was clear. The only thing he wanted to accomplish was to mow the lawn. Other than that he would just live. Come what may. That was enough. It was what he wanted.

An aroma of coffee filled the kitchen. His mother was reading the obituary section of the Delphi newspaper and asked if he wanted her to pour him a cup.

"I'll get it myself," he answered.

"Edna Macek died," said Joan. "Seventy-two."

"I'm sorry. Who's that?"

"She worked with me at the college. Don't you remember? She was the one with the sciatica."

"Right."

Mark reached for the front page and glanced at the photos while his coffee cooled. He saw the usual faces of anguish. He didn't read the articles or even the headlines. He wasn't interested in the news. It was always the same to him. It wasn't news at all. The faces were another thing.

"What's the plan for today?" asked Joan.

"Thought I might try to cut the grass," said Mark, "weather permitting."

"It's supposed to be a gorgeous day," said Joan.

The noise of the gasoline-powered mower allowed Mark to better hear his inner voice. The motor cottoned out all other sound. Its roar wrapped him in a quivering cocoon of his own thoughts. It was oddly peaceful. He pondered the three gray blades of the mower shearing the uncountable blades of grass, blades slicing blades, big blades slicing little blades, steel slicing cellulose, machine slicing nature. And he thought about the stories he'd written. In one way or another they had all been tales of destruction, amputation. He thought that if he were to produce something new it should be about creation, construction, about things and people getting back together, renewal not ruination.

He spied a flash of movement to his left. When he turned he saw a frightened blond college kid wearing blue jeans and a white t-shirt with 'NO MORE WAR' written in red meant to resemble dripping blood. Mark cut the motor.

The undergraduate tried to speak but only stammered.

"Did you just climb over my fence?" asked Mark.

"Yes," managed the kid.

"Why?"

"You're the reason I'm here. I mean you're the reason I'm at Wallace. It's because of your book."

A fan.

"That may be but this is not the college. This is my backyard."

"I know. I'm sorry. I just had to meet you in person. See you up close. They say you never go out. And then I heard the mower so I hopped the fence."

"And here you are."

"Here I am."

"So, what do you want?" asked Mark.

The confused kid looked down at the lawn. Then he tugged on his shirt.

"I don't know. Nothing. Everything. I hadn't thought that far ahead. I just wanted to talk to you."

"What about?"

"Your book. Writing. The world. I don't know."

Joan threw open the back door and shouted at the trespasser.

"You have ten seconds to leave the way you came or I'm calling the police."

"I'm sorry. I don't want any trouble."

"You're not in trouble," said Mark. "But you should go. I don't have anything to say."

The boy tugged on his shirt again, this time pointing to the lettering with his other hand.

"The war. Afghanistan. It'll be Iraq next. You knew about 9/11. What's going to happen? Innocent people are dying. It's not right. You can stop it. They will listen to you."

"I'm not bluffing, young man," shouted Joan

waving the telephone with her right hand.

"There's nothing I can do," said Mark. "I just want to be left alone. Now go. I don't want the police here anymore than you do."

The student threw himself against fence but was unable to scale it from the inside. There was no purchase. He slipped and fell, twice. Mark walked over to the large gate, unlatched it and swung it open. The young intruder sprinted out without another word.

Mark was about to restart the mower when his mother called. He went inside.

"Let me do the lawn," she said. "You've had enough excitement for one day. If they see me they'll move along. It's you they want to talk to. Stay indoors. It's safer."

Mark started to protest but quickly relented. It didn't matter. Let her do it if it'll make her happy, he thought. She thinks she's protecting me. Let her protect.

JOAN

In small town America there's nothing particularly unusual about a woman in her sixties cutting the grass. In general people there take pride in appearances. Joan finished what Mark had started. It took her five more passes and ten minutes to complete the back. She deliberated on Mark while she maneuvered the mower. She wondered if she'd done enough. She couldn't name another man his age who still lived with his mother. It was not natural. She wondered if the time had finally come to tell him she no longer needed him.

It took her an additional fifteen minutes to finish the small front yard and the skinny parkway. Navigating porch, sidewalk and street, Joan thought about Philip. She could keep Mark away but she didn't know if she could do more. She wondered if Philip's sickness was treatable. She worried he was terminal. A small branch appeared in her path so she stopped to pick it up. She left the mower running. She stooped low to reach the maple twig. It was stuck in the hard soil. It had probably been there all winter. Eventually she pried it loose and flipped it into the gutter. As she turned back to the mower she was struck by the horrible realization that if Philip died from a bad liver she had made an irreparable, decades-long mistake. Mark had played no role in Philip's illness. If Philip died now then the Fates had been wrong. And so had she. Pushing the cooling lawnmower back to the garage, its wheels covered in short blades of severed grass, Joan suddenly felt very old and very tired.

Mark had the table set for lunch. He was slicing bread when she entered.

"Sandwiches," he said.

"I'm going to take a little shower first," said Joan, "wash the yard off me."

"The sandwiches will wait," answered Mark.

Joan's thoughts turned to Kate while the water splashed her sore arms. She wondered how Kate was coping. Twice, in the past five years, her daughter-in-

153

law had been pregnant. And she'd lost them each time, one after the next. Now Kate might lose her husband too. That's an awful lot of losing for one person, thought Joan. No amount of money can ease all that pain. Joan mixed the shampoo into her thin graying hair. Her triceps and forearms throbbed. She had overdone the yard work. It's funny how you don't feel the soreness when you're working. It's only when you stop moving. The pain comes later.

Joan smelled the frying bologna as she descended the staircase. From the age of nine Mark's favorite sandwich had been fried bologna with mustard relish. He now made it better than she ever had. She sat at the table. Two tall glasses of cold milk stood waiting. There was a diagonally divided ham and cheese sandwich and a handful of potato chips on her plate. She thanked Mark while she placed the paper towel napkin on her lap.

Joan wanted to say something about the morning's intruder. She wanted to tell Mark he shouldn't talk to such people. It only encouraged them. Mark bit into his sandwich with gusto. She held her tongue. Joan said nothing. She didn't want to spoil his meal.

As they sat in silence—there was no awkwardness in the quiet, they were way beyond that—Joan, out of the corner of her eye, watched Mark devour his sandwich and chips. He was still her little boy. He always would be.

She popped a potato chip into her mouth and shattered it with her teeth. The pieces mixed with saliva and turned to mush, pockets of pulp tried to hide in the ravines of her molars. She took a drink of milk and washed the paste down. The third prophecy echoed in her head. It was Walter's voice. It took her by surprise. It always did. *'The grandchild will be born a monster.'* She shuddered. She looked at Mark. He smiled showing off an uneven milk mustache. He doesn't know what I know, thought Joan. He never will.

KATE

"You're being too hard on yourself," said Rose.

"Am I? I'm raping my dying husband. What does that say about me?"

"It says you're scared."

"It says I'm selfish," answered Kate.

"You're human."

"Too."

Kate asked Rose to consult the Tarot cards.

"The cards won't help."

"I know," said Kate, "I know you can't read the future. The cards are props. I've always known. But at least they're something. You were the one who told me I'd have a child. You told me not to give up hope. You told me to wait. That it would happen naturally. And then it did. Like you said. Twice. But you never told me I'd lose them. You never told me my tiny sons would die in my womb, dead before the first breath."

"Kate, I'm sorry."

"It's not you, it's me. I kept the sonograms. I

155

look at them every day. It's an obsession. I wanted to believe. I still want to believe."

Rose uncorked a bottle of Beaujolais and poured half the contents into a huge glass and handed it to Kate. Kate took a big gulp while Rose spoke.

"My customers are like actors on a stage. But the stage is the universe. The stage is life. And they come to me when they can't remember their lines, when the plot is lost. They've forgotten, for one reason or another, how to act. They're adrift. So, just like in the theater, when an actor can't remember their next line someone offstage gives them a prompt. And they keep prompting them until the lines come back and the play continues. I'm the prompter. I help people get back in their story."

"They put their faith in you."

"And I listen. I keep them going."

"They want answers."

"I give them comfort."

"They want the truth."

"I don't tell them anything they don't already know to be true."

After a second bottle of wine Rose called for a taxi. The two women kissed and Kate, drunk, headed back to North Beach and Philip.

The taxi driver chose Van Ness. Kate looked out the window at the fleeting cityscape but the car's speed, its stops and starts, made her stomach somersault. She focused instead on the cab's registration posted on the back of the front seat. The photo was color, grainy. She couldn't begin to pronounce her driver's long name. There were just so many vowels, so many letters. Kate wondered where he was from originally, what exotic, bizarre land of excess letters he called home, how far in his young life had he to travel to find his way to San Francisco, California . . . to drive a taxi. She had only come from Iowa. But she had been around the world. Twice. And some people never leave their birthplace. Kate thought about Meg and her three children, teenagers now, stuck in Delphi, forever.

Her key wouldn't fit in the lock. She took a step back to adjust her vision and was about to try again when the door popped open and she was greeted by a giant stranger.

"You must be Kate," said the stranger.

"I am," she answered crossing the threshold. She scanned the room until she found Philip. He smiled. He never had visitors. He never received guests. She wasn't particularly worried. She was drunk. She was curious.

"I'm Bradley," said the stranger extending his hand.

"He's Bradley," said Philip. "I just hired him. He's to be my factotum."

Kate was about to gush about what a wonderful idea it was and how nice it would be to have an assistant and that she was sure it would work out marvelously and how he would be a big help to her husband and his interests and how she looked forward to having him around the house. She was going to charm him, maybe flirt a little. But, as she started to open her mouth, she realized she probably smelled like a lush. It was not the first impression she wished to make. At a minimum, mouthwash was needed. In an undertone she excused herself and hurried to the bathroom.

She brushed her perfect teeth and gargled with luminous green mouthwash. She reapplied makeup here and there and brushed her hair. Only then did she exit the bathroom and make an entrance.

"Bradley, please excuse my sudden departure. It couldn't be helped."

Kate crossed the room and kissed Philip.

"I think it's a wonderful idea. Philip, I've been telling you for ages that you needed an assistant."

"I finally listened," said Philip.

"Welcome, Bradley. Welcome."

Because of this stranger's sudden and unlikely appearance and the effects of the Beaujolais, Kate worried Philip was preparing to die. The moment passed. She decided to have more wine.

PHILIP

Bradley was a second-year biology major at San Francisco State. Philip had chosen his résumé from among hundreds. He was the only candidate Philip invited to the house.

Bradley's height surprised him. Bradley was tall, taller than Philip. Philip wasn't used to people being taller than him. Then again, of late, he wasn't used to people. Of course Bradley had heard of the renowned Philip Copeland. Aegis was a household name. Bradley was timid and agitated in the presence of the software legend. He was polite. He was deferential. Philip liked him immediately and told him the job was his. Bradley was given a dedicated phone and told he'd always be on call, night and day. His duties would be whatever Philip needed, whenever he needed it. It was perfect for a bright, hard-working, flexible student. He would be well paid. Money was not an issue. Bradley accepted without asking a single question. He thanked Philip for the opportunity. He apologized for his nerves. And then he ran out of words. The room grew quiet. A scraping sound, outside, broke the silence. Bradley's first official act was to open the door Kate couldn't.

Philip cringed when Kate asked Bradley if he'd like a drink. She was having wine.

"I don't think that's legal," said Philip.

"I'm nineteen, ma'am," said Bradley.

Kate laughed. Philip knew she wasn't laughing at her faux pas; she was laughing at being called ma'am. Philip could tell she was drunk.

Kate was perched, wobbling, wine glass in hand, on the narrow armrest of Philip's chair. Bradley leaned forward from the settee hanging on Philip's every word. He was discussing immortality.

"I have various interests. Athanatos is where my heart and most of my money are at the moment and I thought it might particularly appeal to you," said Philip.

"Fascinating," said Bradley.

"Imagine eradicating death," said Philip.

"Imagine."

"What do you think?" asked Philip.

"Amazing."

"But what is your opinion, Bradley?"

"I don't suppose I have one really. I'm imagining."

"You're a biologist."

"I'm only a sophomore."

They laughed.

After Bradley left, Kate stumbled to the bedroom and fell asleep. It wasn't like her to drink during the day, thought Philip. He wondered whether she was beginning to crack under the strain of his sickness. He hoped he had hired Bradley in time.

Philip poured himself some wine. He wasn't supposed to drink—medications, diseased liver, etc.—but Kate had left half a bottle. And, besides, she was in no position to stop him.

The wine tasted too tannic. He put down the glass after two sips. He could hear his wife snoring. She even snored beautifully.

Philip slipped a notebook from his front pants pocket and opened it. He wanted to jot down a few topics for Dr. Clairday. He had some new ideas. And he wanted Bradley brought up to speed ASAP. But his mind quickly clouded. Meeting and hiring Bradley, playing host, had exhausted him. He understood he wasn't getting any better. He wasn't any stronger. Philip closed the notebook and questioned his commitment to Athanatos. He questioned his motivation. Is it because I'm dying I'm so interested in death? Am I seeking salvation? Will religion be next? He needed rest but was too tired to make it to the bedroom and he didn't want to disturb his wife.

He placed the notebook on his lap and closed his eyes.

He woke an hour later. Kate was still snoring, kitten purrs really. Philip felt better, weak but better. He cursed the wine for the depth of his fatigue. And he dismissed his negative thoughts as anomalous. He vowed to be stronger. He would at the very least project greater strength. Going forward he committed himself to defeating his lethargy through positivity.

That night, after the lights were extinguished and the alarms had been activated, Philip didn't wait for Kate to initiate sex. He assumed the aggressor's role. He got on top. He kissed her forcefully and worked down her uncoiled body, pausing between her legs. He made her feel his long weight as he returned to her open, eager mouth. He spread her thighs and entered her with a single, firm thrust, missionary style, like man insatiable. And he made love to his wife until they came together. Philip may have been sick, but he was not yet dead.

MARK

He was near enough that he could make out the two black tips of its red tongue as they flicked at the air. The snake itself slid slowly. Most likely it wasn't dangerous, thought Mark, looks like an ordinary garter snake. The serpent was in no hurry to reach its destination, wherever that was. At intervals, half-hidden, it stopped in the midmorning sunshine, sometimes for a minute or more, searching the breeze with its tongue, its small brown head darting as if catching a message on the wind. Mark attempted to anthropomorphize a purpose for the snake's twitchy behavior but failed. He'd followed the aimless reptile from one side of the backyard to the other. He'd gotten so close he could have, with little effort, snatched it up from the grass. His shape had created unnatural eclipses. He had made accidental noise. And yet he hadn't frightened it. The snake displayed no fear. If it was aware of Mark's presence it did not reveal its awareness. The slithering stopped when it reached the fence. It had crossed the sizable lawn, a field of short grass with little cover, nowhere to hide. It had taken over an hour. But it stopped at the fence. And it waited. Mark wanted the snake to look him in the eye, to acknowledge his presence, but it didn't. Instead it raised its head, licked the air once again and disappeared into the green. And it was gone. It vanished. It ceased to exist. It must've escaped between the wooden slats, thought Mark. It ran away, legless.

Mark stood, brushed the dirt from his bald knees, and noted the snake had slipped away from the same section of fencing the anti-war college student had vaulted a few months earlier. Mark's mind played with the idea of a backyard portal, a magical wormhole. Perhaps the kid and the creature were breathing embodiments of the same entity. Maybe the inquisitive coed had had his time after all. Mark laughed to himself at the notion that he had just spent the entire morning tracking an indifferent garter snake through the grass but wouldn't give five minutes to an idolizing young student. He really had become antisocial.

There'd been a time when he was happy answering questions. He recalled his days at the student union. He remembered how after graduation he was more than happy to assist the coeds with whatever they needed. And he remembered Chuck. So much had changed. He had changed. Hadn't he? Everything changes. Mark still believed he was being true to his philosophy, that he was living life on his own terms. But he wasn't blind to the fact that, whether because of his book's notoriety or not, he'd become a loner. The few communal outlets he'd had were now fewer. Mark questioned his privacy policy. He thought about Kate. He thought about long nights at the Grill and long walks around Delphi. He remembered Emma. And he thought about his brother. He thought about Philip. Through solitude am I denying myself the full experience of existence? Is isolation making me less human? Is it making me reptilian? he half-laughed. But Mark was perturbed. He was troubled he hadn't said more to the student. He should've invited him inside. He should have been kinder, more human. He vowed to change.

He crossed the lawn and walked toward the door. Looking down he saw a twisted black figure in the grass. Another snake? A family? Upon closer inspection it became a stick of maple, gnarled and lifeless.

The back door opened and his mother called out.

"Mark, I'm heading over to the Purcell place.

163

Do you need anything before I go?"

"No, thank you. I'm fine."

"Well, I won't be long. We can play Scrabble when I get back if you'd like."

JOAN

Joan mainly used the Purcell house as additional storage space. In return she kept it clean, made sure the mailbox was emptied and paid various neighborhood teenagers to weed, mow and trim the property. It was still known as the Purcell place even though, technically, the title was in Philip's name. After Chuck died it was on the market for over a year without much interest. Philip purchased it for Kate, as a gift of sorts. His version of a dozen roses, Joan figured.

Joan stored the Copeland items separate from the Purcell belongings. Her things: old clothes, several record players, tools, a sewing machine, tangled wiring, spare lumber, etc., were kept either in the large hall closet or out in the garage. Those were her spaces on the property. That was her business. But sometimes Joan loitered in the Purcell house just to be by herself and to be away from Mark. Sometimes she needed alone time. And sometimes she snooped.

After Chuck's funeral Kate organized the family possessions she wanted to keep and disposed of everything else. She had been ruthless. As a result the house was mostly empty save a few big pieces of furniture: Kate's childhood bed, the living room sofa, a small round kitchen table with three matching chairs. Kate's closet, however, was stuffed with bursting boxes containing photos, awards, clothing, books and heirlooms. Mementoes. Joan often wondered why Kate didn't want the boxes in California. Why hold on to them from afar? Why keep them here in Delphi, forgotten, gathering dust? Joan reached high and brought down a blue shoe box, size eight and a half. She removed the top. It brimmed with photographs of Chuck. Some were old, blurry polaroids, others were in black and white, most were color, invariably he was smiling. There was Chuck as a baby. Chuck as a boy. Chuck as a teenager. Chuck at Kate's wedding. It was Chuck's life in stills. There were hundreds. Joan was tempted to arrange them in chronological order.

She eased onto Kate's mattress and flipped through the pictures. Chuck had been a handsome man in his youth, she remarked to no one. Muscular, strong features, comfortable. She flattered herself that Chuck had, in his later years, developed feelings, a crush, for her. It was only natural. They had both lost their loves and had been brought closer by their children. He checked up on her. He visited for coffee. But he never once asked her out. They never had a 'date.' Perhaps she was mistaken. Perhaps Chuck was only being polite, neighborly, friendly. Still, she thought she saw something in his eyes. What if they had become an item? imagined Joan. Chuck was so different from Walter. In many respects they were opposites. The simple and the complicated. No, that's too facile. Really, how simple or complicated can one

165

man be? All men are both, aren't they? Her sons certainly were.

And what would Mark and Philip have thought had she found another lover and remarried? How would they have reacted? Joan admitted she had no idea. She admitted she didn't know her sons as well as she had hoped when they were younger. By embracing another man would she be shrouding Walter's memory, tarnishing his name, slighting their vows? Tears blurred her sight. She was too old for romance now. The moment, had it ever existed, had passed. She recalled Walter's smile and his jocular voice. And she missed him. She'd thought they would have had more time together. The best was yet to come. Or so they'd believed. He would be proud of their sons, thought Joan. They are good men. All Copeland men are good. She wiped her eyes. A single tear fell on a photo of Chuck magnifying his image. She dried the picture, gathered the prints, replaced the lid and put the shoe box back high into the closet. What would it have been like to have had another husband? Strange, she thought. Though it would have been better than being alone, she reckoned. Then again, she had Mark. And he had her.

KATE

Multiple consecutive nights of insemination should have had her impregnated by now, thought Kate. And yet her period kept coming, every twenty-eight days, more or less, like a punishment. She was still on the youthful side of forty and there was no reason—according to her gynecologist and his tests—that she couldn't get pregnant again. But she hadn't bargained on Philip's illness. She hadn't accounted for the medications. They've done something to his sperm, she concluded. It's my fault he's sterile. Whatever the reason, he no longer seemed able to provide what she wanted. One by one, month after month after month, she was running out of her egg allotment. It was time to explore alternatives. She wasn't getting any younger. This is as much for him as it is for me, Kate told herself. There was no reason to tell her husband she'd made a decision.

Philip's cheerful change had been overwrought and immediate. Overnight—it seemed to Kate—Philip had become the Philip of old: energetic Philip, the Philip of Aegis and grand plans and crystalline visions of the future. At first she believed Bradley was responsible. She assumed Philip was posturing for his assistant, puffing his chest, playing the alpha male. Later, though, well after Bradley had left for the day, she caught Philip leaning against a table catching his breath and she knew the truth. She recognized then that Philip hadn't changed, he hadn't gotten better; it was all an act. He was pretending . . . for her.

Kate marked how Bradley curved his height as he passed through the doorway. He was taller than Philip, much taller. And he was also much younger. He was young, robust. Not unattractive.

"Bradley. Have a seat. Philip will be out in a moment. Can I get you anything?"

"No, thank you."

Bradley crossed the room and, giraffe-like, lowered himself atop the settee. Kate followed.

"So what are you and my husband up to today?" she asked.

"Not really sure," said Bradley inching away from her.

Kate moved closer.

"Knowing Philip," she said, "it could be almost anything."

Kate laughed and placed her hand on Bradley's shoulder. She left it there.

"Bradley, do you have a girl in your life?" she asked.

"Nope. Not really. With classes and now this job I don't have much time anyway."

"You're just being coy. I bet you have your pick."

Kate ran her hand down the length of his arm and put a finger to her lips. She looked up into his eyes and fluttered her lashes. She felt his breath.

"Mrs. Copeland—"

"Call me Kate."

Philip entered and Bradley stood up. The two tall men shook hands. Kate eyed them both before rising.

"I'll leave you boys to your business," she said walking away.

Kate didn't end the nightly sex sessions. There was still a chance. They were part of her plan. And Philip seemed to enjoy himself.

Kate asked Joan to prepare the Purcell house. She was coming to Delphi. Philip thought it was a splendid idea. Bradley would see he stayed out of trouble.

"Are you sure?" asked Kate. "I'll stay if you think I should."

"No, you go and have fun. See my family. See Meg. Bradley and I will be fine. You deserve a break," said Philip.

"Thanks, I will. I'm looking forward to seeing the old house again and there are a few things I'd like to check on, some things to pick up. Thanks for understanding."

On the day of her departure Bradley offered to drive her to the airport.

"You stay with Philip. I'll be fine with a taxi."

PHILIP

By midmorning the next day two things were apparent to Philip. The first was that he was sicker than he wanted to admit. He was relieved he wouldn't have to pretend to be vigorous for the next day or two. And the second was that he had undervalued everything Kate had been doing for him. He'd forgotten how much work went into living. He'd woken late but tired, and exhausted whatever energy twelve hours sleep had provided showering, making coffee, pouring juice, preparing and eating breakfast. Kate was the one who took care of breakfast. She took care of most things. All these months and she never once complained. She accepted the caregiver

169

role as if she'd practiced for it. He couldn't have asked for more. She really is a wonderful woman and a loving wife, he thought. He knew that in many ways he was a lucky, lucky man.

In the middle of his third cup of coffee—he thought the caffeine would give him a third wind—Philip pictured Kate in Iowa. He wondered what she was doing. He wondered if she'd visited his mother. Had she seen Mark? He thought about calling but resisted. Let her have some time off. Let her forget I'm sick for a day or two. Philip had nothing to do. There were no micro-meetings scheduled, nothing to research, no messages to return. He was bored and tired and alone. So he phoned Bradley.

"Come over as soon as you can," he said.

Bradley attempted to say something in reply. It was garbled. Philip hung up. Twenty minutes later Bradley rang the bell.

"I hope I didn't disturb you," said Philip.

"No. School stuff. I was on my way to the bio lab." Bradley entered, dodging the lintel, and gingerly removed his back pack. "Do you mind?" he said unzipping the bag. "I want to make sure he's okay."

Philip watched as Bradley withdrew a burlap sack from the back pack. The sack shook on its own. Bradley untied the thick knot and reached down deep.

"What is that?"

"A snake," answered Bradley, "specifically a sharp-tailed snake. Oh, don't worry, it's harmless. They're indigenous to the Bay area and surprisingly common. I came across it on my morning run. Almost stepped on it. I was on my way to the lab when you called. I figured you needed me right away so the snake made the trip too. I hope you don't mind."

A squirming rope of rusty scales wriggled between Bradley's fingers. Philip moved closer but not too close. He didn't like snakes or reptiles or amphibians. The aversion stemmed from one hot summer down South when he was eleven. He and Mark spent the muggy days exploring a nearby bayou. Philip tested his strength and his speed sprinting through the swamp, vaulting logs and scampering up twisted trees. Mark lagged behind examining the flora or a frog or lizard, sometimes a snake. Mark insisted Philip touch the critter he'd chanced on or be called a coward. Philip handled the wet, frightened, twitching animals but he never enjoyed it. He wished Bradley would put the snake back in the sack. As if he could read Philip's mind, Bradley dropped the red writhing mess into the bag.

"There's nothing I can do about it now, I suppose," said Philip. "Why don't you take it where it belongs and then come back? I can wait."

"Are you sure? He'll be fine here for a while. He can't get out."

"Yes, I'm sure. But come right back. Do you understand?"

"I understand."

"And, Bradley, next time please leave your biology elsewhere. I don't know what would've happened had Kate been here. It might've upset her. Women and snakes, you know."

MARK

Mark began with short predawn walks, slowly wandering the slate streets of Delphi, swallowing the cold air. Birdcalls and his own footfalls were his only companions. Day by day the walks got longer. Porch lights went out with the rising sun. Inside homes, here and there, a room lit up, bathroom or kitchen, he figured. Mark was still alone but he was again out in the world. He was like everyone else, alone together. He started his matutinal hikes later and later and they lasted longer and longer. He then saw people: mailmen, farm hands, nurses, patrolmen. He passed them nodding in acknowledgement. They looked. They returned his nod. Sometimes from afar they waved. But no one bothered him. By the end of the summer he was taking two walks a day, one post breakfast, one post supper. His ambling, his reasserted presence in Delphi, became routine.

Some nights, late, he went to the Grill and talked with Earl. Most Wallace students had left for the long vacation. Some remained. A few—never the young man who'd hopped the backyard fence—offered to buy him a drink. Then they sat with him and talked, usually not for very long. It was, all in all, thought Mark, not unpleasant. Certainly not the nightmare he'd expected. One night after several free beers he posed for a photo in front of the brick wall. Familiarity devalued his celebrity. And after a while people mostly let him be.

"Mark, is that you?"

"Yes. Kate? How's California?" answered Mark.

"I'm in Iowa. Delphi. Got in last night. Have to leave tomorrow. Just a quickie. Wanted to know if you and my mother-in-law are free for dinner. My treat."

"Sure."

"Great. I'll be there at seven."

The doorbell rang at two minutes after seven. Mark opened the door. Kate stood on the porch in a short white summer dress holding two bottles of wine.

"Well, no need for forks."

Kate laughed entering. "As a matter of fact, no. I ordered pizza from Colucci's. It should be here in fifteen. Hope that's okay?"

They all hugged and made conversation about how long it had been. The pizza arrived and they devoured two extra-large pies: one veggie and one meat-lovers. A lone piece remained uneaten. Kate offered it to Joan but she declined. Mark begged off too. Kate shrugged and gobbled up the last juicy slice in a few quick bites.

"Believe it or not I sometimes miss this pizza," she said chewing.

After dinner and after Joan said it was a shame she wasn't staying in Delphi longer, Mark walked Kate home. Like old times she took his arm. And like old times it felt right. He wanted to keep walking forever. Kate suggested the Grill.

They sat in a booth and talked about Philip and California. Kate asked about Mark's book and his bizarre fame. Just as they were discussing the book's prophecies a coed interrupted for an autograph. Kate picked at her bottle's label and grinned.

"They really think you can divine the future," said Kate.

"Crazy, isn't it? said Mark. "You write a few stories about things falling apart, relationships, trust, shattered glass, toppling masonry and they call you a prophet. Everything falls apart eventually. It's hardly a secret."

Mark settled up with Earl—Kate had tried, unsuccessfully, to pay—and they stood to leave. Kate presented Mark with a liberated label as thanks.

"Oh," she said, "you won't believe this."

Kate reached into her uptown bag and pulled out a faded, creased Old Style label from the eighties.

"I kept it all these years," she said. "I used it as a bookmark when I read your book. Now it's here. And so am I. These used to entitle me to anything. Remember?"

Mark remembered and smiled. He mumbled something about being over served.

"I should go now," whispered Kate.

They walked but did not speak. Countless stars, clustered and solitary, twinkled high in the thick black air. On the porch Kate gave the label to Mark.

"I want you to have it. No strings attached."

Before Mark could say thank you, she shrieked.

"And I've got tons more inside. I saved them all. Thousands! You don't believe me! Come on. You'll see."

Kate dragged Mark over the threshold, into her bedroom and pushed him onto her bed.

"Stay there," she barked.

She rummaged through the bottom of her overcrowded closet until she found a lavender glove box. She lifted the lid. The box held hundreds of old labels. She sat on the bed. She placed the box in his hands. And then she kissed him. Mark fumbled the box and returned her kiss. The labels scattered like fallen leaves.

"You're still so beautiful."

"Am I?"

JOAN

Joan rose worried. The faint morning light had arrived early. She hadn't heard Mark return from taking Kate home. Normally she woke when he came in late. His heavy steps strained the porch planks and the front door locked loudly. But, apparently, she had slept through the noise, through the night. She blamed the wine for her leaden, unbroken sleep.

She wrapped herself in her robe, cinched the sash, toed into her slippers and crept down the carpeted staircase trying not to wake Mark. She was almost to the kitchen when the front door popped open.

"Mom, you're up. I didn't wake you did I?

"No," she answered. "I thought you were asleep, upstairs."

In her mind Joan tried to sum up what it meant that her son, her second son, the writer, was stealing into his own house at the break of dawn after setting off eight hours ago to escort his brother's wife—and *his* former girlfriend—home. Every answer came up negative.

"Are you just getting in?"

"Yeah, we went to the Grill. I must've had too much. I fell asleep at Kate's place."

"You're home now. I was just about to put the kettle on, would you like some coffee?"

"No, thank you. I'm going to try to grab some more shut eye."

She watched Mark mount the stairs and shook her head. "All negative," she said.

Over two large cups of instant coffee Joan replayed supper. They had all been in fine form. The pizza was familiar and the wine tasted expensive. Throughout the evening, though, Joan had wondered about Kate. It seemed her daughter-in-law was too animated, like she was trying to hide something or cover it up. Joan assumed it was something about Philip. Perhaps he's taken a turn for the worse. No, she wouldn't be in Iowa were that the case. What if it had been something else she'd picked up on? She'd been bubbly, attentive to them both, too attentive. She'd been flirtatious. What if Kate had been planning something all along? Mark, my dear boy, is too generous and caring to intentionally hurt his brother, thought Joan. But she wouldn't put it past Kate. If the two former lovers had become lovers again it was at Kate's instigation, concluded Joan. It was her fault. And if Kate and Mark had slept together then the break between her twins was permanent. There would be no reconciliation. Ever. Were Philip to find out, liver or no liver, he'd kill Mark. Or have him killed. Best to pretend nothing happened. Anyway, she didn't know if anything *had* happened. It was none of her business.

Mark came down midmorning. He had showered and was dressed. Joan sat on the sofa reading. He plopped down next to her to get a better look at the book. He quickly dismissed it as trash.

"Well, it kills the time," said Joan.

"Hm."

"What are your plans today?"

"No plans. Walk, think, write, live, nothing extraordinary."

"Will you see Kate?"

"She's gone. Early flight. Probably almost home by now. Said she had to get back pronto."

"What else did she say?"

"Like I said, I drank a lot."

"You don't remember anything?"

"She showed me some things she keeps in boxes in her closet."

"That closet is a disaster. Sometimes the door won't close properly. She'll need to address that someday."

"I need some coffee. Would you like another?"

"No, thank you."

Joan reopened her book and thought about Kate flying west and considered a trip to see Philip. Maybe she could be of some help. But they had been clear. They needed no help. No, she'd just be in the way. It would be better to stay in Iowa with Mark.

KATE

She assessed Bradley briefly. Tall, intelligent, polite, a strong jaw, dark—if small—eyes; and the logistics were manageable. But he was too young, too unassuming, too gawky. He would be troublesome. He was not ideal. He was no Philip Copeland. It would be too complicated. Bradley was deemed unsuitable.

Kate had done the math and the time was right. The house in Delphi waited. She told Philip she'd be back in two days. Bradley asked if he could drive her to the airport. She took a taxi.

Curbside she saw the porch was clean, the grass short and even and edged. The house was small, more shanty than chateau, but it looked presentable, quaint. It was home.

Inside was immaculate. Kate wondered how many hours Joan had spent scouring. She carried her bag into the bedroom and opened it. She removed a few items, some clothes, some wine, her toiletry bag; a gift for Meg. She wouldn't need much. It wouldn't take long. After arranging her things she pried open her closet door. Instantly she noticed her boxes had been moved. Joan, she cursed. Despite the disarray she found the boxes she needed and threw a few keepsakes—a black veil, some photos, an old mauve scarf—into her luggage to bring back to California.

The next day Kate had lunch at Meg's. Her former friend was now officially obese but happy. Her husband was a farmer, soybeans mostly, and they lived a few miles outside Delphi. Money was tight. "What else is new?" laughed Meg. They all ate thick pork sausages and fresh corn on the cob. Dirty children scurried around the property like banshees, screaming and fighting. Every ten minutes Meg warned, "Be nice!" Kate couldn't imagine her child among them. Her life was so different.

She was nervous waiting for the door to open. The imaginary fists in her stomach reminded her of her acting days, just before the curtain rose. It's good to be a little nervous, she'd been coached. It's a sign you care. Use it.

Mark opened the door and made a joke about drinking dinner. Kate hissed a laugh. The wine soon softened the mood and Kate relaxed and had fun. They wanted to talk about Philip. She tried to keep the conversation light.

At the Grill, Kate asked Mark about his book and his fame. True to character Mark didn't want to talk about himself. He mentioned something about everything falling apart and Kate kept suggesting more drinks. Just after midnight she gave Mark the voucher and looked into his eyes. It was time. She leaned in so he could feel her breath and whispered, "We should go now."

Once Mark was in her bedroom it was all over. He returned her kiss like she knew he would and they didn't stop. In a hunger they tore off their clothes. They were like animals. Kate locked Mark with her legs and wondered if he'd ever been wilder. It was over quickly. Kate released him and Mark rolled over onto the labels. They stuck to his skin. They both laughed. Then Kate kissed him again and they slept.

A few hours later Kate woke Mark the way she assumed every man in the world wanted to be awakened. Soon he was inside her again. This time it was slow and long. By the time they finished the first rays of daylight had crossed the room. Kate told Mark she had an early flight. They kissed once more. Mark left.

Kate packed, showered, dressed and called for the plane. Forty minutes later she was in the air.

Philip hadn't expected her back so soon. He thought she wouldn't be home for another day. He pulled her close, leaning on her. Kate asked if Bradley was around.

"He left hours ago. We're all alone."

"Perfect."

And Kate led her husband into the bedroom and showed him she'd missed him. Twice. When Philip was spent and smiling she grinned and slid deep beneath the blankets. She gave Philip a sisterly peck on the cheek and turned on her side.

It had been a very long day. Kate was tired in mind and body. But it was an agreeable tiredness, a solid, satisfying exhaustion. She knew what she'd done. All had gone according to script. And she knew she'd sleep well. Because at the end of that very long day, as her eyelids fell, Kate knew she was pregnant.

2008
HEPATECTOMY

THIRTY-SEVEN WEEKS AND FOUR *days later, at an unlucky hour in a blinding surgical theater of a private hospital within the city limits of San Francisco, California, I was born, ripped without pity or forethought from my mother's womb. The monster was dragged into the light and it—I—drew breath and lived. Thus ends the story of my creation.*

In the beginning—in rehearsals—I planned to describe my hideous birth in a grotesque coda full of howls, carnage and horror. I wanted you to feel *what it's like to become a monster. I wanted to make you squirm. I'd tentatively titled the visceral, bilious epilogue Post-Op. It was to be a sadistic, monstrous proclamation. But I couldn't get it to work. It didn't accord. After many futile attempts I came to the conclusion that the story of my origins was not quite finished; it remained incomplete; it lacked denouement. For example, there is the question of paternity. There is also the matter of the twins' fate.*

*And the truly compassionate among you may even wonder
about the monster himself. I understand. I, more than most, am
sensitive to the requisites of a good story.*

*So, let us continue the tale. Shall we? Let it live a little
longer. We'll stretch our four act faux melodrama into a five act
imitation tragedy. We'll advance back in time from Chekhov to
Shakespeare. Oh, it can work. Yes. I have in me something
dangerous. Ah, and a play within a play. Even better. And,
fear not, I will stay in the shadows, hidden among the sidelights
and the scrims. The stage will be action-packed. You will not
miss my odious presence.*

*Act 5, then, opens when I was five years old. It is the
era of my first memory. It is a good place to stop and start. It is
where my prehistory ends and my history begins.*

*Curtain up. Mark sits at his bedroom desk, hands on
head. His back is toward the audience.*

MARK

"It's no use. I can't do it."

Mark's left hand drops from his head. His ring
finger crashes down on the laptop keyboard
depressing the forward slash key. The screen fills.
//
He does not notice or does not care.

There is a hesitant, knuckled rap on the door.

"Yes."

Joan enters, crying.

"Philip is dying. I have to go to him."

"We are all dying. What makes his death
special?"

Joan ignores the comment. She notices the computer screen and the forward slashes.

"They couldn't go through with the operation. Something was wrong. There was an incompatibility."

"I'm sure he'll buy better doctors or a better, more compatible organ. Always has."

"There's no more time. He's run out of time. This is the end."

"It comes for us all, sooner or later."

"He's your brother, Mark. Your twin."

Mark stands and approaches his mother. He gets close enough to whisper.

"He's a stranger who's stabbed me repeatedly. It is not my fault he's also my twin."

"That's not true. Philip never intentionally hurt you."

"Kate?"

Mark turns his back. Joan searches for words.

"He didn't marry Kate to hurt you."

"That doesn't stop it from hurting."

"It's been twenty years."

"Seems like yesterday."

Mark settles into his desk chair and swivels. Joan goes over to him and places a maternal hand on his shoulder.

"I have to go to him. He's my son."

"Your eldest."

"Birth order is nothing."

"And yet it has made all the difference."

Joan crosses the carpeted room and sits on the edge of Mark's neatly made bed. She glances toward the small window and twists open the mini-blinds.

Sunlight shards angle in. Then she turns to Mark.

"Don't hate Philip. If you need to hate someone, hate me."

"You've got it wrong. I don't hate my brother. That would give him too much power. Like I said, he's a stranger. Two lost souls who once shared a womb. That is all."

"You are brothers. You will always be brothers. If there's any enmity between you it's because of me."

"You didn't give birth to an asshole. That was his choice."

"You don't know the whole story."

"Neither do you, I suspect."

"You don't understand. You—"

"So help me understand."

"I don't know if I understand it all myself."

"We never do."

"I have to go to him."

"That I understand."

"But it doesn't mean . . . you know."

"I know. Go."

"I'm sorry."

"I'll be fine.

"I'm sorry, Mark. I'm doing my best."

"It's me, not Philip. I'm wretched today. And I *am* sorry he's sick. I don't wish him dead."

"I am sorry too."

"Stop it. That's enough apologizing. It's demeaning."

"It can never be enough."

"Mom, you can't apologize for everything that happens in the world. It doesn't work that way. Life is

185

too complicated, too complex, too chaotic and too long. In the final analysis whatever responsibility you bear for whatever you may or may not have done diminishes to the point of meaninglessness. Let it go. We all make mistakes. Life is one great mistake."

"Does that apply to Philip?"

"Yes, it does. But like I said, I'm wretched today."

"There's nothing else to say then. I'm leaving tomorrow."

Joan turns her back to Mark. She exits.

Mark addresses the laptop and slaps the keys with purpose. Text returns. He reads and rereads. He pauses. His hands move headward.

"Awful. Every sentence wheezes. Every word clangs."

PHILIP

In a bright private hospital room, spatchcocked amid machines and wiring, surrounded by beeps, fluctuating figures and precipitous lines, Philip lies, partially raised, under crisp white bed sheets and a thin beige blanket. Kate reading—she is engrossed in *The Hunger Games*—sits to his immediate left in a reclining chair stretched almost to length. Apart from the occasional page turning neither moves. Balletic mute nurses and techs twirl around the machines, like scrubbed angels, medical specters. Philip speaks with obvious effort.

"Who's watching the boy?"

Kate responds without looking up from the book.

"Imelda. I told her I'd be home late."

"You should be with him. There's nothing for you here."

"He likes Imelda. Prefers her, actually. You need me here."

Philip scrunches his face but does not answer. With mild interest he watches the apparitions enter and exit. Time passes, silently. After a period he speaks.

"Tell me again what happened with school."

Kate closes her book slowly. She fights to control her irritation.

"I've told you. Or have you forgotten?"

"I want to hear it again."

"I could turn on some music."

"I want to hear it again."

"All right. But don't get upset. It's nobody's fault."

"Hm."

"You would have been proud. Our boy was such a student, such a little man. He was nervous but he joined in right away. The other kids pointed at first. Some asked him what happened, why he was like that. And then they stopped pointing and stopped talking. They just played. He played. They all played like five year olds. He was so happy to be with other children he didn't even look back. I left without saying good-bye. I didn't want to spoil the moment."

Philip is visibly moved.

"Then, just before lunch, I received a call from

the school. When I got there he was alone and crying. The director said there'd been a problem."

"And?"

"And, she said that our son unfortunately was not a good match for her school. It wasn't going to work. He didn't fit in. She said she was sorry. I tried to ask what had happened but she wouldn't say more. Something about privacy issues. I was livid. And when I left I saw several other parents clinging to their children as if shielding them from our boy, like his condition was contagious. Hard, malicious glares. That part could've been my imagination. Anyway, that was that. I took him home, both of us upset, both of us in tears."

Kate pauses before continuing.

"He almost managed a half day of school. We can try another."

"It'll just be the same."

"Probably."

"How is he?"

"Fine. Forgotten. I told you he adores Imelda."

A smiling doctor, forty, enters. He carries a tablet. He taps it and swipes several times before he speaks.

"Hello, doctor."

"And a good afternoon to you, Mrs. Copeland. Mr. Copeland."

"Call me Kate."

"Kate. Mr. Copeland. How are we feeling?"

"Like death."

"We're doing everything we can to keep you comfortable until a new liver is available."

"And what are you doing to find him a new liver?"

"He's at the top of every list. The next match is his."

"If there is a next one."

Philip scowls at Kate. Kate apologizes to both men without speaking.

The doctor walks upstage to Philip's bed. He removes a penlight from his coat pocket and shines it in Philip's eyes.

"The problem's the liver, not the eyes."

The doctor snorts.

"Hang on to that wonderful sense of humor, Mr. Copeland. It's great medicine."

KATE

The stage slowly rotates revealing two cross-sectioned rooms. The three-walled rooms are divided by a thick, rusty I-beam packed in dirty pink fiberglass insulation, chips of plaster dangle from the edges. The wall's decaying innards contrast with the immaculate state of the two well-lit rooms. Kate enters the left room, her grand North Beach bedroom. Joan enters the right room, the Copeland's homey Delphi living room. They sit simultaneously, each lost in solitary thought. Neither faces the shared wall. Muffled shouts from a young boy can be heard from Kate's side. A door slams loudly somewhere behind Joan. Seconds later Kate reaches for her phone and presses a single button. Joan answers the call.

"Hello."

"Everything's ready. It's all arranged. You'll be here tomorrow afternoon."

"I didn't know what to pack. I don't know how long . . . I'm packed. I'm ready."

"He'll be happy to see you."

"How is he?"

"Not good. Weak. He doesn't have much time."

"Now, now, don't give up."

"Joan, what do I do if he dies? What do I do? Tell me. We have a little boy now. We're a family."

"And how is my grandson?"

"Your grandson will be ecstatic to see a friendly face."

"That poor, poor little boy."

"The little boy is growing like a weed and as rambunctious as ever. We've decided to homeschool him. It's easier."

"I see. I've packed some things, trinkets really. I hope you don't mind."

"Not at all. He loves new things."

"Does he get to see his father?"

"They don't allow children in the ICU. We've skyped once or twice but Philip doesn't like the boy to see him so sick, it's difficult. Besides, Philip left him hours of recordings. So in a way he spends more time with him than if Philip were healthy and home."

"It's hard on all of you. I know."

"It's the hoping that's the hardest. One day there might be a liver and we hope. The day passes without luck and we hope for another during the night. We wake and start hoping again. I used to think hope was helpful, that it was harmless. Now I know better. It's ghoulish. Hope rests on the death of an innocent other. And yet I hope. It's sick. Some unknown, unfortunate being out there somewhere has to die for Philip to live. And that's our only hope. It's a cruel kind of hope, isn't it? Sad and twisted."

"Can't they do anything else while they're waiting? A machine? I read about pig livers being used sometimes. Something?"

"Nothing."

"Nothing."

"A healthy new liver is the only answer."

"I'd gladly give him mine if I could."

"Me too, but I'm not a . . . wait that's it!"

"What's it?"

"You. Mark. Mark can give him his. Mark has to be compatible. They're identical twins. They share the same DNA. Mark can save Philip. Mark is the answer!"

The stage abruptly goes dark.

JOAN

After a moment or two the lights return without warning as quickly as they'd been extinguished. They seem brighter than before. The stage glows. Joan's mouth is agape. It is her turn to speak. She composes herself.

"You may be right. He should be a match."

"I am right. I don't know why we didn't think of it before. All these years."

"But what about Mark? What about *his* liver?"

"It'll grow back. They just take a portion. The liver grows back. Doctors do it all the time now. Live organ donation. Mark will be fine. They'll both be fine. Philip will live!"

"That is the best news."

"Why didn't we consider Mark earlier?"

"They have been apart for so long we forget."

"I guess."

"Just because Mark's a match doesn't mean he'll be able to donate does it?"

"I assume he'll have to be tested first. They'll want to know he's not diseased, not an alcoholic. The liver has to be healthy. He'll have to be cleared."

"And he'll have to consent."

"Yes."

"The same DNA isn't always enough, is it?"

After she asks the question Joan rises from the sofa and inspects the staircase. She returns and sits satisfied. There is a moderate pause and then Kate speaks.

"DNA isn't everything, no. But it's the most important part. He'll be the perfect candidate. Don't you think?"

"I'm not a doctor. And I'm certainly not Mark. It does seem promising."

"Is he there? Is he at home? Put him on the phone. I have to talk to him."

"I think it's best if I broach the subject."

"If you—"

"I know him better than anyone."

"I suppose."

"And if he consents—"

"If?"

"Should he consent we'll go first thing to the hospital in Des Moines and have him tested. You have my word."

"No, I mean . . . yes, but you're already coming out tomorrow. The plane. The best doctors in the world are here. Have him come with you. It'll be faster . . . safer."

"You may be right."

"Are you sure you don't want me to speak with him?"

"No, this has to come from me. They're my boys."

"Okay. I'll get in touch with Philip's doctors. And call me as soon as you've talked to Mark, please."

"I will."

"Joan, get him on that plane."

"I'll do my best."

The call ends. Kate hops up and hurries out of her room. Joan slumps, her chin falls to her chest. She waits. Then she raises her head and turns it toward the vacant stairway.

MARK

The scene opens with Mark and Joan sitting shoulder to shoulder. A single spotlight illuminates their faces and nothing else. Gradually, as they converse, the spot's circumference expands and, at a pivotal moment, their location is disclosed. Joan speaks first.

"I can't imagine a world without Philip. It won't be the same."

"No it won't."

"It makes me happy to hear you say that. Sometimes I worry that you and your brother never liked each other very much. And I blame myself."

"No one's to blame, Mom. We're different people with different lives. Little more than elementary school pals. Liking him has nothing to do with anything. We once shared a past. That's the extent of it."

"When you were born . . . since you were twins . . . I expected—"

"What? You expected us to finish each other's sentences, maybe become famous boy detectives before marrying beautiful yellow-haired twins? You expected us to be best friends forever? You expected we'd have some sort of special, unbreakable, lifelong bond just because we shared the same amniotic sac, just because we're cracked from the same egg?"

"Something like that."

"It's fiction."

"Family is not fiction."

"That's an unconnected issue. I'm saying twin relationships are not exceptional. We are not special. It is a myth perpetuated throughout history by lazy hacks. Twins are siblings, nothing more and nothing notable, certainly nothing special. A little less common is all."

"You and Philip were very close as children, very close."

"I would venture that most children within a

certain age range are close before the age of twelve. Twins are no different. You—and everyone else—always saw the similarities first. Philip and I saw the differences."

"Maybe we're all guilty of not seeing the whole picture."

"Perspective is slippery."

At this point the spotlight's perimeter widens to reveal that Mark and Joan are seated in a private aircraft. Mark occupies the window seat. The shutter is up. After a beat, a tall, attractive female flight attendant interrupts them.

"We'll be landing in about two hours. Is there anything I can get for you?"

Joan requests white wine. Mark declines refreshment. The flight attendant leaves with a smile and Mark speaks.

"It's been ages since I've been anywhere."

"I know. It can't be easy. But I am grateful. And so is Philip."

"He's that sick? It's real this time?"

"Yes, according to Kate."

"Kate, yes."

The flight attendant brings Joan's drink and asks if they would like anything else. She retreats toward the cockpit. Joan swallows and then speaks.

"Mark, there's something I need to ask you."

Mark gazes out the window. They are crossing the white-topped Rockies.

"Yes."

"I don't know how to say this."

"Just say it then."

195

She takes another sip of wine.

"Philip needs a liver. You are his twin. You might be able to save your brother. Kate wanted me to ask you if you would."

"What?"

"Save him."

"Give him my liver?"

"A piece. Kate says it'll grow back."

"You begged me to come and say good-bye to my dying brother, but you really just needed a donor."

"Kate says—"

"Kate says. Kate says. If Philip wants some of my liver he can ask me himself."

As the last word hangs between them, the cabin lurches from turbulence. Mark lowers the shutter. Joan clings to his shoulder and the spotlight goes dark.

PHILIP

"Thanks for coming out. Kate told me all about her scheme. I'm sorry. It wasn't my idea."

"You don't have to apologize. You haven't asked me for anything."

"Mark, I can't. Even if I wanted to—which I don't—I couldn't. And I wouldn't. Also, I've been cautioned that it's unlawful to solicit internal organs."

Philip strains to laugh. Mark explores the bright hospital room. He takes passing interest in the machines and their lights and their noises.

"What does this one do?"

"Every so often it washes my blood."

"Clean blood is good blood."

"The orange light means it's on the rinse cycle."

Philip again tries to laugh. It sounds like a dry cough. Mark motions toward the machines.

"You're really a mess."

"Tell me about it. I've spent the last half decade trying to find a way to live longer, maybe forever. And here I am wasting away like an ordinary schmuck. You wouldn't believe the crap I've been funding: lengthening telomeres, uploading brains, injectable nanobots, you name it. And it's all bullshit. Too little, too late. For me anyway. I conned myself into believing I was helping people, but really I was just trying to save my own skin."

"And now I'm supposed to save you. Is that the idea? I'm supposed to be the great savior."

"Not mine. I'm waiting for a liver. It could come anytime, from anywhere. I'm not asking you for a damn thing. In fact if positions were reversed, I doubt I'd let them carve me up for you."

"Yes you would."

"Don't be so sure."

Mark continues his tour around the large room. Nurses enter and exit without interacting with the brothers. At the end of his circuit, Mark sits in the chair next to Philip. He moves it closer. He pauses before asking Philip a question.

"Do you find it strange that Dad wrote a book about livers and now you're dying because of one?"

"I do."

"Me too."

There is a medium to long pause as Philip summons the strength to speak.

"It gets even weirder. Dad wrote a book on the liver and you wrote a book about things falling apart. Years ago I should've put the pieces together: liver falling apart. I should've seen the writing on the brick wall, so to speak."

Mark laughs and looks at his thin, jaundiced brother who attempts a smile. The grin comes out crooked, forced.

"Are you in a lot of pain?"

"Not really. They tell me I'm on a great deal of medication."

Mark raises his head and notices Kate peeking through the wide glass window. Philip sees her too. Kate waves.

"She doesn't deserve this. She's been by my side the entire time."

"You don't deserve this either. Nobody does."

"Don't be so sure."

"I should go. You should be with your wife."

"Mark, for whatever it's worth, whatever happens, I'm glad you came out. It's good to see you again."

"It's good to see you too. I wish it could've been under better circumstances."

KATE

As Mark exits Philip's room the lights dim leaving a weak disk of light on a weaker Philip. Mark closes the door gently and is immediately confronted by Kate. The stage rotates slightly to bring them into the center. Philip is still visible upstage. Expressionless, he watches his brother and his wife talk. He cannot hear what they are saying.

"I don't know how to thank you, Mark."

"I haven't done anything."

Kate takes hold of his elbow.

"But now you've seen him. You see how sick he is. He's dying. He's your brother, your twin brother. You have to help. You have to."

"I don't have to do anything. And, for the record, your husband agrees with me."

Kate shakes her free hand toward Philip.

"He doesn't know what he's saying. The man is disappearing. He's out of his mind."

"I think he seems quite lucid considering."

She grabs his other arm.

"Are you saying you *won't* help him?"

"I'm not saying anything yet. Not yet. A few hours ago I left Iowa for the first time in decades just so I could come here and pay my respects to my dying brother. That was hard enough. And now everybody wants a piece of me. You all want me to play the hero. Well, if I know anything it's that I'm no hero."

"You can be. It's up to you."

"Forgive me if I'm a little overwhelmed."

Kate removes her hands. She takes a half step back and composes herself.

"You're right. I'm sorry."

There is a lengthy, uncomfortable pause before

Mark speaks.

"It doesn't seem real."

"I know. It doesn't, does it? You know, I've felt this way for so long ago I forget that it's not normal."

"He was always so strong, so goddamned confident."

"The confidence is still there even if the strength is gone."

"No disease can obliterate that, I guess."

Kate smiles and moves closer.

"Mark, nobody can tell you what to do but you can't fault me for telling you what I think you should do . . . what I'd like you to do."

"No, I can't fault you for that."

"He's my husband. And I would do anything to save him."

"I know."

"Don't you still love me even a little?"

"That's not fair. That is not fair. Don't use that against me."

"What else do I have?"

"Nothing."

"Nothing?"

Another moderate pause. They turn and look through the glass window at Philip. Then they pivot and face each other. Mark takes Kate by the arm.

"Kate, we don't even know if I'm a candidate. This could all be academic. A waste of breath and time. Let's see whether I qualify first. Okay?"

"Okay, that first."

Mark exits with long slow strides. Kate fixes her hair and enters Philip's room with a fake smile.

JOAN

The scene is the North Beach condominium living room. Joan and Mark are discussing Philip. Both appear uneasy in the penthouse. At various intervals mother and son glance stage left toward the closed bedroom door. They stop and listen. They meander about the room gingerly handling artwork and photographs. Mark sits awkwardly. Joan speaks first.

"I won't tell you what to do. It is not my place."

"No, this one's on me alone."

"It doesn't mean you *are* alone, Mark. Whatever happens, whatever you decide, I'll be here."

"I know that. And I appreciate it."

"I am your mother."

Joan sits next to Mark on the settee.

"If Dad was here he'd tell me to march down to the hospital and demand they take my liver pronto . . . without anesthesia."

"Probably."

"And, apart from the anesthesia, he'd be right, wouldn't he?"

"I don't know."

"Dad was right a lot."

"A lot, but not always. Nobody's right all the time."

"You're not going to tell me I have an obligation to my brother? You're not going to cry and beg and shame me into saving his life?"

"No, I am not."

"Why not?"

"I have my reasons."

"Such as?"

"Such as: how do you decide what's best for your children when all the options are bad? Such as: how does one choose between twins? Such as: how often must a mother's love be tested? Such as: you are an adult. I have done the best I could. I raised you and kept you safe. But you are a man now. This is your decision. It's out of my hands. Is that enough?"

"Enough."

"I don't mean to seem insensitive, Mark. I just can't protect you from this. It's been a long time. I'm old. I can't."

Mark stands and strokes a smooth bronze abstract sculpture. In a general way it resembles Walter's urn. He loses himself in thought for a moment or two before speaking.

"One of the pamphlets the doctor stuffed into my hands describes the ethical concerns related to live organ donation. It mentions donor autonomy, conflict of interest, freedom from coercion, a bunch of considerations. But it says nothing about family. How do these criteria apply when the recipient is your brother, your twin? Can a twin ever be autonomous?"

"I don't know. It's complicated."

"Ah, maybe I won't even be accepted. Maybe I've spent too much time indoors. Had too many beers with Earl. Maybe my liver is damaged. Maybe I'm not well."

"We'll know soon enough."

There is an offstage thump and a cry. Joan and

Mark look to the closed door. Joan speaks first.

"He's awake."

"I'll go."

"No, let me. He's better with women."

"Like all Copeland men."

Joan laughs and kisses Mark on the cheek before exiting through the door. Mark sits on the settee, breathes deeply and closes his eyes. The stage goes black.

MARK

Kate bursts through her wide front door as the stage lights are thrown on. Mark sits where we left him last scene. He has not moved. He opens his eyes and Kate is already in midsentence.

". . . you'd be here. I thought they wanted you at the hospital. The doctor said they were waiting to speak with you. Anyway, I'm happy you're here. Making yourself comfortable? Is grandma in with him?"

She motions toward the bedroom door. Mark nods. Kate places her handbag on the bureau and removes her light jacket and hangs it. She slips out of expensive pumps and in one easy motion slides them aside with her foot.

"Can I get you anything?"

"How is he?"

"Philip? The same. Worse. I don't know. It's tough to tell."

"No, I meant the boy."

"Oh, him! You've seen him. Healthy as an ox. He's got more energy than the rest of us put together."

"Psychologically."

"Mentally? He's five years old. They're all crazy at that age. If you mean his intellect, they tell me his IQ is high."

"Smart enough to know he's different."

"Definitely that."

"How is he coping?"

"Five year olds don't cope. They just live. He knows he doesn't look like everybody else. And he doesn't like it. Who would? But he doesn't sit around thinking about it. He plays. He runs. He screams. He has tantrums. He's five."

Mark thinks about what she's said before he speaks.

"Five years old and this is the first time I've seen him."

"Time flies."

"It does something."

"Don't take this the wrong way, but I always thought you'd have wanted to see him before this . . . that you'd have come out years ago."

"I don't get out much."

"I thought in this case you'd want to make an exception."

"Why?"

"I don't know . . . curiosity?"

"Because of the way he looks?"

"No, of course not."

"Because he's my nephew?"

"Closer."

"What then?"

Kate sits beside him and pauses for a long time. She looks him in the eye and whispers her next line.

"Because you're his father."

Mark stands. Kate leans back in the settee shocked to see that Mark is shocked. She continues.

"Probably. It's impossible to know. It's either you or Philip . . . of that I'm certain."

"How?"

"He was born nine months after we were together in Delphi."

She pauses again and looks him up and down.

"You never considered it? You never once did the math?"

"Never. Not once."

"You used to be so perceptive."

"Does Philip know?"

"Oh God no! Do you think I want to kill him?"

"Why didn't you say something before?"

"Why would I?"

"So I would know."

"I figured you *did* know. Or rather, I figured someone as smart as you at least suspected. Besides (she laughs) back then I thought you could see the future."

"Great Pan is dead indeed!"

"What does that mean?"

Mark sits.

"Nothing. Nothing at all."

Joan's loud laugh is heard offstage. The child guffaws in return. The lights fade.

PHILIP

Philip's brightly lit hospital room early the next day. He appears weaker, yellower. Joan sits in the faux leather chair next to his bed. It is pulled close. As ever, hospital employees flit about the room without disturbing the conversation.

"Promise me—no matter what Kate says—you'll continue to support Athanatos."

"Of course, dear, whatever you want."

"I may have to die but maybe my son can avoid the fate."

"Don't talk like that. You're not going to die. Not yet."

"Don't be so sure."

Joan begins to cry. She wipes her tear-stained cheeks and apologizes.

"I'm sorry, Philip."

"For what? Crying?"

"Everything."

"Me too, Mom. Me too."

Joan stands and attempts to hug her son but gets tangled in tubes and wires. The muddle provides needed comic relief. Joan begins to cry anew.

Mark enters.

"I can come back later."

Joan answers, dabbing her eyes.

"No need. I was just leaving."

She turns to Philip.

"I'll be back."

"Thanks."

Mark sits on the chair before realizing it is too close to the bed. He stands and repositions it a few feet away. Then he sits back down and faces his brother.

"She's having a hard time with this."

"She? What about me?"

Philip tries to laugh at his own joke but is too sick. Mark laughs for him.

"You always have to be the center of attention, don't you?"

"Seems it's been my lot."

"And your mission."

There is a medium pause. Philip's lopsided smile turns to a frown. His words sound feeble and angry.

"Mark, you don't think you're superior to me because you have no money, do you?"

Mark smirks. He waits a beat before answering.

"No, I am superior to you because I'm younger, smarter and better looking."

"Anything else?"

"I have a healthy, functioning liver."

"You're hitting below the belt."

"Above actually. And yet according to your doctors it is medical fact. The results are in. My liver is perfect. It's a match. I am a match. I have the green light."

Mark pauses briefly before continuing.

"Philip, I can give you some of my liver if you want it."

Philip sighs and rasps before speaking.

"I told you I can't ask."

"I'm not asking you to ask. I'm asking whether or not you want it."

"I don't know."

"You don't know. Do you want to die?"

"I don't know that either."

"Fuck, Philip, I'm trying to be the bigger person here."

"You always tried to be bigger."

"Do you want me to say no?"

"Do what you want. That's what you're best at anyway."

"Kate was right. You are out of your mind."

"I'm being honest."

"You're being stupid . . . and selfish."

"The great thing about dying is it frees you from giving a damn. It frees you from performing."

"You're still alive. And nothing but death frees you from performing. Trust me, I've tried."

KATE

The North Beach condominium. Kate tinkers with the expensive coffee machine perched on the counter in her deluxe kitchen. She presses buttons again and again, over and over. Nothing happens. Watching her, Joan sits in a chair at the head of the kitchen table. Kate is distracted and frustrated. She speaks without looking at Joan.

"There was a time I thought I knew Mark better than anyone in the world. Blasted thing! The Mark I knew would revel in the idea of helping his brother. He would have relished the opportunity. Ah, got it."

"That was a long time ago. People change."

The machine kicks on. Water drips slowly into the sleek pot. Kate faces Joan before speaking.

"Not that much."

Joan speaks dreamily.

"More than twenty years."

Kate sits at the opposite end of the long glass table. She plants her elbows and crosses her hands.

"Isn't there anything you can say to him?"

"I've done all I can."

"Maybe the doctors—"

"Mark doesn't trust doctors. That would only make it worse. No, I think we have to let him decide for himself what's best."

"And you don't think he's being selfish?"

"I think we're all guilty of that."

"You people and your pointless philosophies! Your stupid, stupid ideas! I'm sorry, Joan, but if it was me we wouldn't be having this conversation. My husband—your son—would be better already."

"I know."

"You don't have to make excuses for him."

"I'm not making excuses for *him*."

"He never grew up. That's his problem. He's still a child."

"Mark is a good man. You're being unfair."

"Am I?"

"Yes, and you're acting as if he'd said no. He hasn't said no yet. Don't beat him up for something he hasn't done. You'll regret your words."

"He hasn't said yes."

"No, he hasn't said yes."

"And you don't have an issue with that?"

"I'm waiting."

"Philip can't wait. Do you want him to die?"

"That's—"

"Not fair?"

"No, it's not."

"Nothing about this is fair."

"You're right."

There is a moderate pause. Kate looks toward the coffee machine and then the closed kitchen door before speaking.

"I don't want to lose my husband. You of all people should appreciate that."

"Oh, Kate, dear, I do."

"And it's my fault."

"It's no one's fault."

"I ordered it. I bought it. I served it to him. I watched him drink it. I poisoned him."

"But you couldn't have known."

"What does that matter?"

"It should. It does."

"It doesn't change anything. It doesn't make him better."

"No."

"How do I tell my son I killed his father?"

"You didn't—"

"But I didn't mean to, really. Trust me."

"Oh, Kate."

"What difference does forgiveness make? What difference will it make for him? What difference does it make for any of us?"

The two women freeze, allowing Kate's questions to swirl in the air above their heads. They remain motionless as the words ripple and disappear.

JOAN

Match cut. The previous scene continues. With a shrill (recorded) whistle, mimicking a boiling kettle, the fancy coffee machine announces the brew is ready. Kate composes herself, rises and speaks.

"Two sugars, right?"

"Yes, two, please."

Joan tries to change the tone and subject of the conversation. She fails.

"You have a beautiful place. And San Francisco is lovely."

"Lonely?"

"I said lovely. It is lovely."

"Sorry," says Kate carrying a steaming cup to Joan. "I hear the sinister in everything. It's hard to keep positive."

"You're strong, Kate. And you've got your boy to look after. It may not be easy but you'll get through it."

"One way or another."

"Yes."

Kate sits with her cup of coffee. For a minute or two the women do not speak. It is as if they are each waiting for something to happen, something outside their control. Joan revives the dialogue trying to find a cheerful topic. This time she fails herself.

"My grandson certainly adores Imelda."

"She's the only person outside the family he trusts."

"Poor little guy. Such a burden."

"He's a trooper."

"Every time I see him my heart breaks. The one eye. That tiny, adorable monocle."

"It's plastic, you know."

"His head. I don't know how his little neck can support it."

"His head is actually normal sized. The shape of it makes it look bigger than it really is. He's used to it. After all it's the only head he's ever had. He never complains. He's still just a baby really, trying to live the best he can."

"And despite his . . . his challenges, despite it all, he has the biggest, the happiest, *the* most genuine smile I've ever seen."

"He's a sweetie all right. He'll outlive us both."

"Such a cross to bear."

"One he'll have to bear without his father to help."

"We don't know that."

"Unless Mark steps up, it's the one thing we *do* know."

"Even if Mark agrees, there is no guarantee Philip will survive."

"What a horrible thing to say, Joan."

"You're pinning all your hopes on Mark. It's idealistic. I'm just saying—"

"I know what you're saying. I know very well

what you are saying. And, believe me, whatever you can imagine I've imagined a thousand times. But it's quite another thing to say it out loud. And about your own son."

"You should be prepared."

"Were you?"

"What?"

"When Walter died, were you prepared?"

"No, that was an accident. I couldn't have prepared myself."

Joan pauses and adds shakily.

"There was nothing I could've done."

"Would it have made it any easier?"

"Perhaps. No. I don't think it would have."

"Why would it help me?"

Joan's eyes begin to glisten.

"It's doing something."

"Not for Philip."

"No."

"Let's do something to help Philip then. Let's talk to Mark . . . together. Okay? It may not work but we'll be doing something."

"Yes, you're right. You're right. We have to do what we can. We need more than hope."

"Agreed. And, until then, only good thoughts. Okay? The bad, should it come, will be bad enough. There's no need for previews."

MARK

While Kate and Joan are agreeing to persuade Mark to

consent to the surgery, the twins continue their conversation in the hospital. Philip speaks first.

"I do not want to die."

"On that we agree."

"That you don't want me to die or that you don't want to die?"

"Both."

"Is that why you can't decide? Are you afraid?"

"Maybe."

A nurse bumps into Mark. He nods to her and moves out of her way before resuming.

"Maybe, but that isn't it."

"Mm."

"It's not you either, though you're a much bigger factor than the fear of death, if that makes you feel any better."

"A bit."

Mark pauses before his speaks.

"If you—if anyone for that matter—were trapped inside a burning building screaming for help I would run in and try to save you in a heartbeat, without a second thought. There would be no question. But here, now, with the consent forms, the counseling, the deliberation, the hushed voices, the doctors and policies and procedures, it's—"

"Like they're taking the fun out of it for you."

"Kind of, yeah."

"Tough break, everybody looking out for your welfare."

"It doesn't seem noble. It seems clinical."

"It's a hospital, Mark, not a firestorm."

"Dad went the right way: quickly, no warning,

no time for incrimination or rumination.

"Nobody goes the *right* way."

"Just like nobody lives the right way."

"We do the best we can."

"And it's never good enough."

"Hey, I'm supposed to be the depressed one."

"Then let's change that."

"Huh?"

Mark moves close to Philip and whispers in his ear. Philip looks confused at first but then grudgingly nods. Mark speaks in a loud voice meant for the nurses. He overacts.

"I know it must be difficult in here with all these people constantly milling about. At least you can take solace in the knowledge that your final minutes will be among others."

Philip hides a crooked smile and the brothers wait and watch. After a pause, Mark hams it up again.

"Yes, dear brother, privacy is precious."

The last nurse heads for the exit. Philip waits to speak until her generous rear end is swallowed by the door.

"So?"

"Go ahead."

"You have to say it like you mean it."

"Really? You're really going to make me say it."

"Yes."

"Please Mark consent to the hepatectomy."

"Too dispassionate, more emotion."

"Help me, Mark. I'm dying. I beg you."

"Better, but sell it."

"Don't let me die. I'm your brother. I love you.

215

Help me."

"You're acting."

"I'm dying."

"You're bad at both."

"Dammit, Mark. Give me a big, fat, fucking chunk of your fucking liver."

"Hardly believable, but, yes, fine, you may have my liver. Heck, I barely use it anyway."

Philip gathers his strength before delivering his line in a high pitched southern accent.

"My hero."

PHILIP

Same scene, third part. Although Philip is half mocking him, Mark blushes after being called a hero. The twins do not speak. After two beats, a deluge of supernumeraries floods the room as if they'd overheard Mark's consent and are hurriedly preparing for an immediate double surgery. As expected they perform their tasks wordlessly without interacting with Philip or Mark. The stage lights soften and Philip appears healthier, less jaundiced than before. Mark stands and the brothers shake hands to seal the agreement. Philip wraps both his intubated hands around Mark's right hand and says:

"Thank you, Mark. Seriously, thank you."

"There's no need. I want to do it."

"Still."

There is a slight pause before Mark asks:

"What happened to us? In a pod one minute,

split the next. Peas. Bad metaphor, I know. But we used to be so close. What happened?"

"Life."

"Is life so long?"

"Too long or too short. Now I sound like you."

"Long, long ago . . . before there were differences and distances between us."

"When we were but boys."

"Seem like different lives, don't they? Boyhood and adulthood."

"They are."

"I remember. I remember we used to do everything together."

"I remember we used to work our asses off to stay in Dad's good graces."

"Oh, he wasn't that tough on us."

"Easy for you to say."

"What?"

"You were his favorite."

"You're nuts. If anything it was the opposite."

There is a medium pause before Mark speaks, imitating his father.

"The liver, you might be interested to learn, was seen by the Greeks as the seat of emotion."

"Stop it. You sound just like him."

"Contrastingly, the Japanese, historically, have considered the liver as the seat of intentions."

"That's him."

"One may posit, therefore, whether or not, in the broadest imaginable sense, the liver, has been, from time immemorial, a cultural Rorschach test, if you will—"

"Yes."

"—a hepatoid mirror reflecting humanity's underlying fear of the unknown."

"Perfect."

"Apples and trees, you know."

"Yes, more things falling apart."

Mark laughs.

"Touché. Entropy is yesterday's news."

"I missed you."

"Me too."

"And thanks again."

"And thank you."

"For what?"

"The money."

"What money?"

"My book didn't sell that well. And yet my publisher never complained, never dropped me. Kept sending me big checks. All these years. It had to come from somewhere."

"You knew?"

"I guessed."

"Mom?"

"No, never said a word. Remember, I used to be able to see the future."

"Yeah, me too."

Blackout.

KATE

Kate and Joan are in the North Beach living room. Joan is on the settee. Kate nervously paces about the room. They are waiting for Mark to return from the hospital. Eager to confront him, they cast furtive glances toward the door. They both appear in better spirits, tense but determined. They seem closer, more familial, united in anguish. Kate speaks.

"We may only get one chance at this. Maybe we should have a plan."

"Like a script?"

"No, nothing that calculated or phony. More like general agreement on who should speak first, our demeanor. That kind of thing. Some tactics.

"Like an intervention."

"Closer."

"Well I think I should go first."

"Fine."

"Alone."

"Alone? Don't you think it's better if he sees we're both on the same side?"

"Alone . . . at the beginning. There's a bond between a mother and child. He'll feel less threatened. I'll appeal to his family loyalty, his sense of duty. Let me try that first."

"Fine. But I'll be listening from the kitchen and I'm coming out with guns blazing if things go sideways. And I'm going to hit him with everything I've got: love, ego, guilt, shame, tears. I'm not going to hold back, Joan. I want you to know that."

"I understand."

In unison they look to the door as if they've heard the same sound. The door handle does not move. After a pause, Kate zigzags to the settee and sits. Fidgeting, she suddenly appears less confident.

She struggles to find the correct placement for her hands; eventually she pins them to her lap and clears her throat. She speaks shakily.

"Joan, there's a possibility that in the course of the conversation something might come up that you should probably know in advance."

"I'm sure—"

"No, please let me finish."

"Of course, dear."

"I don't know how to say this, particularly to you. It's embarrassing. Oh, Christ. Here goes. Your grandson may not be Philip's."

"I don't—"

"He may be Mark's."

"How?"

"The important thing to remember is that this shouldn't distract us from the task at hand."

"But I don't understand."

"Oh, there's nothing to understand. I was with them both around the time of conception. It was a slip. That's it."

"Does Mark?"

"Yes, Mark knows."

"And Philip?"

"No."

"No?"

"No, he doesn't know. I don't know for sure. It never seemed relevant. And just the idea could kill him. Why would I risk telling him?"

"Then why tell Mark?"

"I thought it would help."

"But it didn't."

"No, not yet."

"I see."

"Joan, I'm sorry. I thought you should know. I don't want anything to jeopardize—"

"I understand."

"Can you still do this?"

"I have to."

"He's still your grandson. Nothing's changed. He's still a Copeland. It's the same exact DNA. It has to be one of them. There was no one else. I swear."

JOAN

Another match cut. At first Kate looks to Joan for reassurance. She wants to hear that the revelation doesn't matter and that everything is all right. Joan's face is inscrutable. After a minute Kate can no longer bear it and turns her head. Joan's face remains blank. Kate appears to be struggling to say something but emits only a weak sigh. She stands up from the settee and moves to the other side of the room. Joan finally speaks, pensively.

"The same DNA."

"I didn't mean—"

"No, you're quite right."

"I'll tell Philip as soon as he's well. I promise."

"That's none of my business. Your secret is safe with me."

"My secret."

"We all have them."

"Some worse than others."

221

Joan stands and turns her back to Kate before speaking.

"Years ago, I almost told your father something I probably should have. I regret I didn't. Things may have turned out differently."

"My father?"

"Don't worry. He is innocent. He plays no role in this. He was a sympathetic ear, that's all. Your father, Chuck, was a kind man."

"I don't understand."

"I should've confessed to him but I didn't. I was too afraid."

Joan turns toward Kate and continues.

"There's nothing to be afraid of anymore."

"Joan, I—"

"When Walter died . . . as he was dying, as we waited in the waiting room, a piece of my past flashed through my mind, an old memory returned like a thunderbolt. I'm going to sound crazy, I know. This memory, this vision, predicted my husband's death."

"What?"

"Please, dear, let me finish, please. A long time before the accident—a horrible, horrible night, in a terrible, terrible city—Walter and I had our futures foretold by some of his graduate students. They were dressed as the Fates. Oh, that doesn't matter. It was supposed to be a joke. But they were right about Walter. They were right. He died as they had predicted."

Joan begins to tremble.

"Joan, I have a good friend who calls herself a psychic and she says—"

"I told you. Crazy. Say what you want but they were right. And it gets worse. There were two more predictions."

"They came true too?"

"One. They said my grandson would be born a monster."

"It's a birth disorder."

"The only prediction that hasn't come true is the one I feared most. It is the one I've worked hard to avoid. But I can't do it anymore."

"What is it?"

"One son will be the death of the other."

"Joan, it means nothing. It's so general. It could mean anything."

"It means Mark will die giving Philip his liver. Or that Philip will die from Mark's liver."

"Or Philip will die because Mark refuses to donate his liver."

"They'll die no matter what I do."

"We all will, I'm afraid."

They hear a noise at the door.

"It's Mark!"

"It's Mark."

The knob turns slowly. Kate dashes into the kitchen. Mark enters.

Joan greets Mark with a hug. She guides him by an elbow to the settee where they sit.

"Mark, we have to talk."

The lights fade.

MARK

The scene opens in Philip's hospital room, very early morning. Mark rests on a gurney next to Philip. Both are dressed in hospital gowns. Nurses and orderlies appear and disappear. The twins share a final exchange before they are to be separated and prepped for the operations. Mark begins in midsentence. He is half laughing.

". . . and then she says the girls—graduate students in *history*, mind you—also predicted that one of us would kill the other. And she was completely serious."

"A truck killed Dad, not a turtle."

"I said the same thing."

"So she tried to keep us apart?"

"For our own safety."

"All these years."

"Decades."

"She sabotaged our relationship. I wouldn't have thought she had it in her."

"I don't know. It couldn't have been that difficult. We were always going to go our separate ways. We were always similar, but different."

"We've certainly had our differences."

"None insurmountable though."

"Except that you slept with my wife."

"Huh?"

"First. I mean you two were together first."

"But you won her in the end."

"Yes, I did."

"And I always loved you."

"Me too."

"I hope this works out."

"The procedure?"

"Yeah, I hope it makes you better. Yellow's not your best color."

"It'll work, don't worry. You're not afraid, are you?"

"It's not fear."

"What then?"

"Don't know."

"We've got the best doctors in the world. It'll be over before you know it. Try and enjoy the experience. Maybe you'll want to write about it one day."

"Maybe."

Mark pauses before continuing.

"I once had an idea in my head to write a short story—an O. Henry/*Twilight Zone* kind of parable—about a man who is so afraid of dying that he's physically unable to leave his house. The poor guy is absolutely convinced that certain, instantaneous death awaits him outside. For a time he manages quite well. He invites friends over. He has everything he needs delivered. He works and socializes over the Internet. He lives. Not an exciting existence, mind you, but he lives. But as he ages he becomes more and more superstitious, more and more afraid of impending death. He becomes more hermetic. He begins to believe the Grim Reaper himself is coming for him and will, at any moment, knock on his triple-bolted security door and tell him his time is up. Packages and mail pile high on his porch. He bans visitors. He grows gaunt and gray. Then one day the doorbell rings. He considers ignoring it but curiosity gets the better of him so he peers through the peephole and sees a familiar face in a delivery uniform. It is a delivery man he recognizes, a guy who's brought him supplies for years. So, slowly, hesitantly, he unlocks and opens the door. The deliveryman smiles, hands him the parcel and says, 'Here you go. It's curtains. For you.' Hearing this, our recluse drops dead on the spot. The end."

Philip laughs weakly. Mark doubles over.

"That's funny."

"Whatever happens, we lived as best we could. We lived."

PHILIP

Match cut. Nurses begin to disconnect Philip from the monitors. They loop wires around their wrists and roll away machines. Philip speaks first.

"No, they can't take that away from us. They can do whatever they want to our livers but they can't change our past."

"This brush with death has made you more philosophical. It's an improvement. You used to be too practical."

"I've come to the realization that pragmatism has carried me as far as it can."

"Dad is rolling over in his grave."

Philip tries to laugh, then becomes serious.

"Do you think he'd like who we've become?"

"Dad? I think he'd love us. But I don't think parents ever really understand their children, at any age."

"It'd be nice to have him around. He'd be able to take care of Mom."

"What are we going to do about her?"

"No idea."

"Maybe she should move in with you."

"Bite your tongue."

"Sorry. But a part of me worries that without her Fates she'll have nothing to keep her going. I worry she'll let herself get old and give up."

"I don't see her ever giving up. Too stubborn."

"I hope you're right."

"We'll see. Plus she's got a grandson to corrupt."

"That poor kid."

A tall, bearded doctor steps between the twins. He says it is time. Mark reaches over and the brothers shake hands.

"Have a good operation, Philip."

"You too, Mark."

"Feel better."

"Oh, I'll be right as rain once the new liver takes hold. And when this is all over, when your liver is back to full strength, I'll buy you a beer at the Grill.

"I don't think they recommend liver patients drink alcohol."

The doctor shakes a long admonishing finger.

"Right. Point taken. (whispers) I won't tell if you won't. We'll say we're going to shoot pool.

227

Exercise. That'll be our cover story."

"I hate being the bearer of bad news but the Grill is no more."

"Earl?"

"Sold it. Said he'd had enough. Rumor has it it's going to be a boutique for children's clothes."

"What about the wall?"

"I imagine they'll do something to it: cover it up, tear it down, sandblast it into newness, who knows?"

"We'll just have to find another place for that beer then."

"Yes, we will."

Orderlies spill from the wings and wheel Mark out of the room and offstage. Doctors and nurses huddle around Philip hiding him from view. A hand appears from the medical scrum and violently yanks on the curtain. This hides them all. There is a brief pause and then blackout.

KATE

The final two scenes play out on a rectangular thrust stage. Kate and Joan sit in the center of the thrust, which is pushed far out into the audience. There are large, metallic twin doors over which a sign reads 'Surgical Theaters.' The doors lead to the raked main stage and two operating rooms, which for the time being are hidden in the darkness, stage left and stage right. The room occupied by the women is reminiscent of the waiting room where Walter died, though updated and more upscale. Bibles and tissue dispensers abound. A thin, flat-screen television occupies half a wall.

Kate stands suddenly and paces around the room.

"Years I've waited for this. Every day, for years, we hoped and prayed that today would be the day we'd get news of a liver. And now that day is here. I never would have guessed these last few hours would be the worst."

"It'll be over soon."

"You don't know that. What if there are complications?"

"They would've told us."

"Do you mind if I turn on the television?"

"No, dear, go right ahead."

"No, I can't concentrate. I wish they would tell us something."

"Do you want me to go ask?"

"We should stay together."

"I'll stay."

Kate sits in the chair beside Joan.

"I've dreamt about this for a long time."

"About the surgery?"

"About us. About us all being a family, all of us healthy, being a normal, happy, healthy family. All of us."

"It's a nice thought."

"It would be too cruel if it were taken from me now, don't you think?"

"Yes, I do."

"Yes. Too cruel."

After a moderate pause, Joan speaks.

"Kate, there'll be a recovery period. Things may not be so easy. What if I stayed to help out until Philip gets better?"

"That's kind, Joan but—"

"I promise I won't get in the way. Just an extra pair of hands."

"Thanks. We'll see. Let's get through the surgery first."

"Of course."

"Between you and me, I've been thinking—once Philip is better and all—that maybe we'd—the whole family—move back to Delphi. Iowa would be a great place to raise our son. You'd be there. And Mark."

"Sounds wonderful."

"It does, doesn't it? Don't say anything to Philip though. Or Mark. This is the first time I've said it out loud."

"You have my word."

JOAN

The waiting room scene continues without a break in the action. Stage left and stage right—the two operating theaters—are now faintly lit: Mark is on the left, Philip on the right. After a beat or two a spotlight shines on Mark's face. A moment later a second identical spotlight is trained on Philip. The lighting circumference of each spot is fixed tightly on head and upper torso. The stage is adequately raked so the audience can see the patients' expressionless faces. It is impossible to tell the twins apart. Masked doctors and nurses, featureless silhouettes, moving in the shadows, surround them. They work slowly and methodically. Neither Joan nor Kate acknowledges the lights or the action.

Joan stands and walks to the coffee machine.

"Would you like a cup?"

"No, thank you. I'm nervous enough."

"There's decaf."

"No, thank you."

Joan pours herself some hospital coffee and adds two sugars before returning to her seat. There is a pause, then she speaks.

"I have been so stupid."

Kate ignores the comment.

"This is my fault."

"It's nobody's fault. It was an accident."

A short nurse enters through the tall twin doors. She removes her mask and explains that Mark's procedure went well and he should be out of surgery soon, while Philip's is taking a little longer than normal. There is nothing to worry about, she adds. It's a complex operation. Mark will be in recovery in a few minutes and she will return when Philip's surgery is over.

Joan thanks her for the update. Kate sighs with relief. They both watch the nurse exit through the imposing doors.

"My poor, poor boys."

"She sounded upbeat, didn't she?"

"Thank God we're all together."

Joan takes a sip of her coffee and stares at the clotted sugar resting at the bottom of the cup. She turns away from Kate and whispers an aside:

"A tortoise to the skull."

"Did you say something?"

"No, dear. I didn't."

"It'll be over soon."

"Yes, I hope it will."

After a beat Joan and Kate abruptly stand and gaze woodenly toward the operating theaters. In unison they look stage left, then stage right, then back again. The nurses and doctors attending to Mark and Philip are now moving with immediacy bordering on desperation. Chests are thumped. Paddles appear. Someone calls for oxygen. Another shouts 'Clear!' The twins remain motionless. Joan and Kate stare upstage without reacting. The spotlights go out one by one. Mark's first. Philip's second. Then the lights of the thrust stage, those illuminating the watching, waiting women, fade slowly. The curtain falls with a thud.

OP REPORT
CURTAIN CALL

LEGEND SAYS THE ONE-EYED *are blessed with second sight, that they can see the future. I cannot. And according to certain Islamic sects, a monocular Anti-Christ will herald the end of times. It will not be me.*

I have no future. I herald nothing. I see only the past.

I was born with cyclopia, which means that I have only one eye, one orbital socket and my nose is almost nonexistent, an indentation. I am grotesque. Cyclopia is terribly rare in human beings; it is slightly more common—for some unknown, unstudied reason—in sheep and cats and birds. My doctors boast that I am the only case in recorded history to have survived more than a few weeks, a combination of rotten luck, my mother's will and my father's money, no doubt.

So, whatever else my grandmother or the Fates might have been wrong or right about, whatever my mother believed or hoped for, whatever the brothers Copeland privately thought as the colorless anesthetic gas clamped their senses, the fact is I was *born a monster. That much is empirically true.*

Death's executor, however, is often more veiled.

Mark died in recovery. He sailed off on a sea of sedatives and never returned. My father died too, and, though he lasted three weeks longer than his brother, he never emerged from his coma. Joan, the only grandparent I ever really knew, passed away in her sleep twelve years later, leaving Kate, my mother, with the last first-hand word on my beginnings.

Genetic science has advanced considerably since 2008. A simple test now exists to determine paternity between identical twins. I have never sought the test. As far as the world is concerned, Philip is my rightful and legal father. End of story. Though there are moments, I must admit, that I have my doubts. In the final analysis, I suppose, it doesn't make any difference whether my father is Philip or Mark or some primordial deity. It doesn't change a thing. It doesn't change what I am.

Rereading, I fear my drama has been too harsh on the women. Perhaps I was kinder to the men because they had the misfortune to die before their time. I never knew them. They are legend. The women, however, survived. They remained. They endured. That was their only real sin.

I branded Joan with infamy. I needed an antagonist and she was an easy target.

I portrayed my mother as an opportunist merely because she loved me.

In their own ways my forebears all did their best (my mother still tries) to pass down what they thought was the truth, to share what they considered important. Mark did finish a second book. I found it hidden in Grandma's attic. A tale from the grave. My father bequeathed hours and hours of video to view, 'when the boy is old enough to understand.' And, for years, my grandmother regaled me with stories, many of which appear on these pages. I have enough fodder for a hundred lifetimes, too many conflicting stories. They are my inheritance.

In the preface to his book on haruspicy my grandfather, Walter, wrote: 'History is always evolving. It changes as we change. To confront the past is to alter it.'

I have elected to live like this, confronting my past, revising my origins, spending my days resting my thick, asymmetrical head on expensive pillows dreaming of a world before I was born, changing it. That is all I have. Monsters have no future. My life is but a defective regeneration of an ancestral past.

So, indulge me. Let me give it another go. Yes? I will try again. Stay. Allow me an alternate version . . . versions. Shall I? We'll continue playing. The game is not yet over. Yes, once more. Call it an encore. Okay? Let me begin again. I'll get the box. Maybe there's something I've neglected. Ready? Good. I believe there is a great past ahead of us.

I AM A MONSTER . . . .

Larry Francis is the author of four previous novels: *Halves*, *Derrida's Toast*, *Heteronymous Bosh* and *Belief in the Great Gear After*. He lives in France.